THE MIDNIGHT KINGDOM

THE MIDNIGHT KINGDOM

ALICE HIGHTOWER

Apex Books

Contents

for K. T.

who whispered music into my soul
and taught me how to sing

I

I don't often wish for much. I'm fairly content. I've worked hard to accept my lot in life, playing the cards I've been dealt with a smile on my face. But in this moment as I'm hurtling toward the earth, I wish the tree branch I'd chosen for my afternoon nap had been above softer ground.

Squinting my eyes shut tight, I brace for the impact... but the impact doesn't come. Opening my eyes, I see the sky above me, almost frozen in time, growing no further distant as the seconds march on. A glimmer ripples across my vision, and then I feel myself falling again. With a hiss and a thud, I hit the hard earth, my shoulder and hip absorbing much of the blow. Groaning, I roll to my other side, gingerly pressing fingertips into the sore flesh.

Before my assessment can continue, a loud commotion meets my ears and my foggy brain assembles a reasonable conclusion - something has startled me awake, causing me to lose my normally perfect balance and send me crashing to the ground.

But what happened with my fall? Was I still dreaming? Am I ill? Shaking my head, I chalk it up to the extreme heat of the summer sun, and quickly duck for cover.

Without regard to pain, I move as quickly as I can to the nearby riverbank, disguising myself in tall grasses. Crouching low, I peer at the scene rude enough to wake me from my peaceful slumber.

A gilded, ornate carriage is stopped on the nearby road and footmen whirl about, struggling to gain control over a horse that gone wild. Tossing its head frantically and pawing at the ground, the horse snorts and whinnies in painful bursts. Well-dressed women are being bustled out of the carriage, rushing away from the impending danger. A second horse, harnessed with the first, grows increasingly anxious.

I've never been a hero; the opposite, morelike. In a lot of ways I'd like to leave these aristocrats to their fate; stranded with lame horses, a broken carriage, and a few bloodied footmen. But it's probable that they'll spot me at some point, coming to the river to wash wounds or fetch a drink. In fact, my coin purse is a little light these days... I might be able to avoid robbing them altogether if I can convince them to pay me for my assistance. If not.... Well, I can feel my knife still tucked neatly against me.

Deciding on a course of action, I quickly test my bruised side, ensuring nothing is broken. Satisfied, my eyes scan the river quickly, a smirk settling onto my lips. I know just what to do. But who would I be if I didn't add a little drama?

I pluck a nearby flower from the ground by its roots, dip it into the river, and hurriedly wrap it in broad leaves. I roll along the riverbank until I am within two long strides from their party, injured ribs jolting with every rotation. Pulling myself even with the injured horse's side, I press two fingers into my mouth and let out a whistle louder than a banshee's scream, then spring from my cover. There is a split second of quiet, and I take advantage of their stunned faces.

I cannot prevent a small grunt of pain as I leap onto the stallion, and I roll myself over its flank and onto the animal's back. Pressing the soaking wet flower neatly against its nose, I hold on for dear life while it tosses its head, tries to bite me, and the once-again alert footmen begin shouting and reaching for their weapons.

This had better work.

I don't have to wait long. A few seconds more and the animal's eyes begin to droop. I scramble to unsheathe my knife and slice through the leather holding the two horses together. The mare rears and races into a nearby field, shattered pieces of wood dragging behind her. The stallion beneath me settles, the tossing subsides, and he slinks to the ground. I slide off, wincing as I hold the long wooden rails steady until I can set them down. Satisfied, I begin to turn, but the cool prick of steel against my throat halts my movement.

"Drop your knife!"

I comply, the blade sinking neatly into the dirt at my feet, and my eyes take in the scene. Four men, swords drawn and pointed in my direction; one pressed just under my chin. Realizing the severity of my situation, I assume a look of innocence. "Now, gentleman... is this the way to treat the one who just saved your horse... and all of you?"

"What's she going on about?" One of them tries and fails to hide a whisper to a comrade.

"I haven't any idea, but you can bet we'll find out. I'm certain the King would love to know who's here trying to take off with the princess."

My eyes flit from the carriage, taking in its ornate design, to the women huddled fifty meters down the road dripping in silk and pearls, to the crest on the chest of the men pointing their swords at me.

Fuck.

"My esteemed gentlemen, please. I had no idea who you were at all. I am but a simple traveler, and I have experience with wounded horses. I only sought to assist."

"Oh yeah? What've you done with the horse, then?"

I shift slightly, attempting to gesture to the flower on the ground before his nose, a sickly purple liquid oozing from the petals. "Those are the blooms from a *somnus aeternam*... surely you've heard of it? Deadly to man - but to a horse? It simply puts them to sleep." Feeling bold, I lift my hand and point to the horse's foot. "See there? That green spot in the horse's pad: your horse has stepped on a poisoned thorn. It must be in excruciating pain. Let me make a poultice for it. I can draw out the thorn and relieve him of the poison; you will need to have him walked the rest of the way home, but I daresay he will not be lame nor dead." Drawing myself up to my full impressive height, I add, "I'm sure the

King would be grateful to you for your efforts in returning not just his horses, but his princess home safely as well?"

The sword tip wavers.

"How do we know that what you say is true?"

I shrug, relaxed. "Go look for yourself. My dear sirs, I would never wish ill upon our great King or his family, but it matters not to me whether you accept my help or not. If you can find someone else to solve your predicament, please do. I shall return to my home, thank you very much."

I turn away, feigned nonchalance my best defense as I move to step beyond the cluster of guards- but a flurry of color catches my eye. "Don't! Please, don't go!"

A young woman is rushing towards me as fast as her voluminous skirts allow. Two other women follow her, looks of confusion and alarm on their faces. The guards drop to their knees, heads bowed to her, though each keep their sword expertly pointed in my direction and I'm sure their eyes are still only on me. *Ah. This must be the princess.*

When she reaches me, she dips her head into a practiced curtsey, made less charming by the blush on her cheeks and the heavy breathing from her exertion. "Please."

She lifts her head and makes eye contact with me, gasping a little. Irises the color of whisky and amber glitter beneath a waterfall of dark, curled hair. Her eyes scan me quickly, lighting over my trousers, shirt, and vest, then landing on my hair, pinned tightly to the back of my head. "But... you're a girl!"

I smirk, bowing low before her. "That I am, your highness. But do tell me how that bears any mention at a time like this?"

She frowns, shaking her head of this thought and gestures to the horse. "Can you really fix him?"

I can hear concern evident in her voice. "I can."

"Then do it."

"It would be my pleasure."

Before the guards can convince her otherwise or the scandalized looks on the faces of her ladies-in-waiting cause her concern, I rush away from the swords and towards the horse again. Kneeling in the dirt, I lift the hoof and examine the vivid green thorn wedged into soft flesh. I click my tongue, gently touching the horse's nose. "Don't you worry, boy. I'll get you fixed up."

I find my knife in the nearby dirt and carefully pick it up so as to not cause any alarm. The footmen act at once, swords lifting towards my throat again and the princess inhales her breath sharply. Holding out a steadying hand, I speak calmly. "I'm not going to hurt him, but I cannot touch the thorn myself. Let me use the knife to pry it out." I keep my eyes trained solely on the princess, holding her gaze steady. She is clearly my best advocate for getting out of this without being arrested or killed, and a reluctant sense of authority over the footmen.

She nods and I smile at her, the footmen lowering their swords. Returning to the horse's side, I lift up the knife, slide the tip into the thorn's base, and using my other hand as a fulcrum, gently pry the massive thorn free.

"Ah ha!" I shout gleefully and rise, a three-inch-long thorn speared perfectly onto the tip of my knife, but my elation is instantly snuffed out. It melts, oozing down the knife and I drop it just before the substance reaches my skin. Black-tinged blood bubbles from the hole in the horse's foot, and I realize with a sickening lurch in my stomach that I was wrong. I felt so certain this was a simple thorn from a Lion's Fire bush, but the blood trickling towards my feet is not ... normal. I've only seen this once before, many years ago in my childhood village, and that memory will never leave me. My mother had barely been able to save the boy, and only luck had ensured the antidote was within her medicinal stores.

The horse begins to stir, legs twitching and kicking. It won't be long before he wakes fully, and this poison causes excruciating pain. Panicked, I race to the river, scanning the rocks in the middle. *It has to grow around here. It has to!* The late afternoon sun is glaring, and sweat trickles down my brow, blurring my vision. I stare hard into the waters, desperately searching for the antidote.

Time slows to a stop, and I'm ready to turn around in defeat and accept my fate when a sliver of bright red catches my eye. *Yes!* I leap into the river, ignoring the shouts behind me, and swim full speed towards the small bush blooming on an island in the middle of the river. The current is strong and my body is screaming with effort. My bruises are battered as I bump along the rocks but I swim hard, forcing myself to continue. Finally, the red berries are clutched in my palm, and I push off once again for shore. Scrambling up the bank, my clothes are torn, my hair has come undone from its hold, and my fingers are numb, but I lay the berries in the dirt and smash them with a small stone. I scoop up the pulpy bits and dirt around them, spit into my hands, and work it into a rough paste. Silently whispering prayers to the goddess, I mash the paste into the wound.

The horse rights himself fully, wildly tossing his head and pawing at the ground with his wounded foot and I scramble backwards, out of harm's way.

"Curaidh!" A clear, crisp voice rings out and the stallion's head snaps up, seeing the princess. She holds out her hands, eyes set firmly into his. "Curaidh. Settle."

I hold my breath as she approaches him, one finger extended towards the tip of his nose. The horse tosses his head once or twice, but calms, and with all the tenderness of a mother and her child, the princess touches her fingertip to his nose. "There you are, boy." She smiles, and presses her nose to his, breathing deeply.

There is a still sense of awe around this little group standing in the bright sunlight on the side of a river. I watch carefully as eventually the horse rests his foot against the ground.

The breath I let out is loud and I even chuckle a little. The princess turns and her gaze falls on me. It is intense, fearless, and calculating... and I find myself shifting uncomfortably in my stance.

When she speaks, it is quiet but full of strength. "Thank you for your service. I shall always be grateful."

I scratch the back of my neck, unnerved by her focus. "You'll need to fix the carriage's whiffletree... I had to cut the leather for the mare over there and she broke off a bit of the shaft when she ran. Your horse can't pull right now so one of your footmen will need to lead him and I suppose that means you'll have to find another horse. None of this I can help with."

One of the ladies in waiting looks scandalized, and leans over to her counterpart, not bothering to lower her voice. "She's caused us as much trouble as she claims to have saved us! Better to have simply killed the beast and moved on."

"Eugenia!" The other woman giggles and swats at her arm.

The princess's shoulders tighten and she turns towards the women. "I will deal with you later." Her voice is as cold as steel and they visibly shrink back. I cannot help but smirk at them, but when she turns back to me, I assume a look of somber responsibility.

"Please forgive them. They obviously have no concept of the value of this horse, nor do they apparently possess an understanding of how important Curaidh is to me."

I smile at her and bow again. "It is of no consequence, your highness. Now if you'll excuse me... I really must be going. There is a village about an hour's walk up the road. You should find assistance there." I point, then look up to the sun's position in the sky. "Do be careful though. I hear a well-known bandit is known to prowl these roads after sundown." Letting a bit too much irony to drip through my words, I waggle my eyebrows at the women behind the princess. "Wouldn't want to get caught up in something nasty, now would you?"

Facing the princess once more, I bow deeply, and I can hear her gasp. "You're hurt!"

Quickly glancing down, I can see the bruises and scrapes on my shoulder are visible through a tear in my clothes. "'Tis nothing, your highness. I am quite alright. If I can heal your horse, do you not expect that I can heal myself?"

She frowns, looking anxious. "Can I not pay you for your services? You..." Trailing off, she gestures to my attire. "Your clothing will need to be replaced even if you refuse to see a trained healer."

I tip my head and look at her. "I suppose I could accept."

The princess motions to a footman, who tosses a small pouch

of money at me. I catch it quickly then right myself and spin on my heel in the opposite direction.

Her voice rings out behind me, calling to me. "What is your name?"

I let the smirk slide back over my lips and I look back to meet her eyes. "I'm afraid, your highness, that is something I simply cannot tell you."

She blinks a few times, narrowing her eyes. "Then tell me this! Why are you dressed like a boy?"

I gesture to her overwhelming getup. "Because dresses are uncomfortable infernos that inhibit movement. How would I have swooped in to become your hero today, if I had been wearing... that?"

And then I take off into a sprint, her laughter ringing behind me like a clear, crystal bell.

2

It's been hours. Where the hell am I?

I swear I was only an hour north of the village of Parlamer, but three hours have passed since my heroic deed of the year and I'm still waiting to see any signs of a town.

Frustrated and in pain, I look down at the bundle of herbs clutched tightly in my palm.

Guess I'd better make do with present circumstances.

Finding a flat spot to sit in the shade of a broad tree, I lean against the trunk with a sigh of weariness. Grateful to be off my feet for a few minutes, I close my eyes and allow myself a quick respite.

Eventually the dull aching grows and I get to work.

Nearby rocks help me beat the plants down to a soft, soggy mess, and I gently rub the blend into my sore and tender flesh. I'm managing, but the more I flex and move, the more certain I am that my ribs are bruised.

Pulling off my vest, I bite down on the edges of a seam and pull, ripping the fabric along its threads. Satisfied that I can fashion a sort of bandage from its now tattered shape, I work to wrap it around my middle... a task not easily done.

On the fourth attempt, I throw it into the dirt, swearing loudly - first from frustration, then from pain.

A mocking laugh rings out from behind me and I whip around,

pulling myself into a crouch, fists at the ready. Without my knife, I'm feeling far too vulnerable.

"Don't be a fool. I'm not here to hurt you." The voice is old and scratchy, humor dripping from every word. "Not that you'd be hard to take down at the moment."

Out from behind the tree steps a tiny old woman leaning on a stick almost as crooked and straggly as she is. Large eyes the color of midnight sea blink at me like butterfly wings under a mess of grey hair, and she cocks her head to stare at me unabashedly.

"You want some help?"

"I don't need any."

"So you're a liar, too! And not a very good one." She shakes her head, moving closer. Pointing at the torn fabric on the ground, she gives me a stern glare.

"Hand it over. I'll hold it in place so it doesn't keep slipping."

The woman is beyond tiny and frail. I'm not even sure she could hold something firm enough for me to pull on, but she's right. I do need the help. And I'm certain I can fight her off if she's stupid enough to try anything.

"Alright... thank you."

Gingerly reaching for what's left of my vest, I pluck it off the ground and hold it out to her.

Standing beside me, she pins the wrapping into place, moving about me as I turn, and secures it firmly with an expert knot at the top.

"There. That's better!" Stepping back, she admires her handiwork, then shoots me a skeptical glare. "How'd you learn to make that balm for the bruising?"

I give her the same, safe answer I give everyone. "My mother was a healer. She taught me a few things."

The woman's eyes flash widely for a moment, a look of sheer surprise - and maybe fear - fluttering over her face. But it quickly settles into a neutral expression and she nods to me.

"That would do it, then. Well. Good day."

She turns to go, and I call out to her. "One minute, please!"

"Yes?"

"Please tell me where I might find the closest inn. I am in need of lodging, a bath, and a hot meal."

"Yes... you are." Her hawk-like eyes narrow at me as she examines the ruinous state of my clothing, but then she grunts and tips her head down the road.

"It's just another twenty minutes' walk before the castle town comes into view. Those mountains there are all you need to follow."

My eyes follow her gesture, confused. Surely there were no mountains near where I was resting today... have I traveled so far?

"I thank you for your kindness. How can I repay you?"

The old woman smiles a toothless grin at me, eyes sparkling. "You already have."

Holding up one of my large silver coins, she laughs her same taunting laugh, then turns to go.

I can't help but gasp, feeling under my clothes urgently to ensure the two coin purses I carry are still present and weighted. Pulling them out, I can see their contents basically intact... but the newly acquired payment from the princess is missing one silver coin.

Watching the old lady walk towards the horizon as the sun nears its daily death, I can't help but laugh. It's not every day you meet someone like her.

*****

"I said, I like your cloak!" The woman leans down, talking louder the second time. "You're all flushed, though! Might be better if you take it off..." She bats her eyes, but I draw the stolen fabric tighter around me and down the last of my mug, wishing she'd leave me be. Only able to find this simple lightweight garment hanging in a window, I have to make do with it to cover the tattered state of my attire until morning when I can secure more items for mending - or at this point, a new outfit all together. Scowling into the empty mug, I finally look up into her eyes.

"Do you usually drink this much? You must have a very impressive constitution." The barmaid leans across the table, breasts practically oozing over the top of her dress as she taps one long finger against the rim of my empty glass.

"Do you make a habit of barging in on other people's personal lives?" I sneer at her, and she dons an offended expression, slinking away from the table. "Bring me another!" I shout after her, and she visibly tenses at my words.

I sigh, slumping even further into my seat. On a typical evening, I'd be far more flirtatious in my approach, drawing her in until I could revel in the pleasures of her touch, lips, and the comfort of a warm bed to sleep in at night. But all I can see in my head tonight is the thorn, melting into a sticky black substance.

I visibly shudder, mind racing as I recount the events from earlier today. That thorn is from a plant that only grows on the western side of the mountains in the country of my birth, hundreds of miles away. What in the world was it doing here? And how did it end up in the hoof of a horse? It seems far too bizarre for it to be a coincidence, knowing how unique the thorn is: thin enough to go often unnoticed in larger animals, it affects its victim slowly, seeping its poison over time into the bloodstream, silently doing damage while the infected creature carries on with life unaware until one day, death comes quickly. And yet... if discovered and you pull it out, the thorn's barbs break off backwards, flooding the bloodstream with a rush of poison that kills within minutes if the antidote is not received.

The Great Northern River has its birth in my village, the violent ocean erupting into the earth, carving its way inland. The seas are too rough for fishing and the weather is too cold for farming so most of the families I remember from my childhood either herded goats and sheep or hunted. No one would have any reason to visit if not for the hot springs that dot the rocky slopes of the mountains just beyond. There, in the tributaries that flow from the mighty river's wrath, unusually warm waters grow the Cara plant, with broad, silvery green leaves and vivid red berries. Many healers would make the arduous journey to my village every year, seeking out the berries for their extraordinary healing properties. Only growing in warm waters during summer months, Cara berries are found in only a few places across all of the known world.

It's too unbelievable to think the thorn could have made its way into the horse's hoof by accident... but then why did the incident occur so close to one of the rare locations of the Cara plant? Why create a crisis within arm's reach of the antidote? Was it intentional? Or did someone's hubris get in the way?

My mind is racing, exploring the possibilities. Sitting up in my seat, I walk my fingers over the worn table, retracing the afternoon's events in my head. Maybe my presence unknowingly foiled a plan. Maybe the poison wasn't supposed to cause any problems until they had reached their destination. Did I somehow insert myself into a sinister plot involving a princess?

A dull thud pulls me from my thoughts; a different barmaid sets a new mug of ale down onto my table. "That'll be six bittens, please." She seems indifferent, so I plaster on my most charming smile in the quest for more information. I pull a silver coin from my purse and slide it across the table, touching the tips of her fingers. Her eyes widen, and she looks at me alarmed.

"Sir! I mean, Miss! That's far too much!"

"Good service is hard to come by, and if you shake your head any more you'll ruin those pretty little ringlets in your hair."

She stutters, blushing, and I wink at her. "Say... what do you know about the King and his daughter?"

Her brow narrows in confusion, thrown by the sudden change in subject, but the poor thing follows along. "What do you mean by daughter? Which one?"

Where exactly am I? I'm not one to wander aimlessly. I do my research. I plan my movements, carefully choosing which roads, towns, and royals to steal from. I learn politics and local gossip, never allowing myself any more than petty thievery until I'm sure of my movements. I've been to each of the six kingdoms left in the Great Empire. I'm supposed to be in Venezia... where the king has four sons and one daughter said to be more beautiful than the sun. Unless he's secretly hiding a second daughter somewhere...

A gnawing feeling of worry settles into my stomach.

Keeping my eyes on the drink before me, I pitch my voice low. "He has more than one?" I take a sip from my mug, trying to play it casual, but my apparent lack of information has the barmaid slightly unsettled.

A nervous trill of laughter ripples off her lips and she looks around. "You... you don't know? Everyone knows of King Alexander. He has twelve daughters!"

The ale in my mouth sputters out of my lips and I scramble to wipe my tattered sleeve across my face. "Twelve?"

The barmaid cocks her head at me, unsure. "Yes, miss. There are twelve of them from four different mothers. The king's got a bit of a reputation, you see. But that all stopped when the last one of them was born. Her mother died then, and the King's closed our borders ever since."

She chews her lips... hands wringing tightly together in front of her. "How exactly did you get here, miss? There's been no outsiders in Gormliath for twenty-two years."

A sudden wave of nausea flows over me, my lips opening and closing a few times as I try to grasp her words. "This is... Gormliath?"

"You don't look so good. Let me get you some water!" The barmaid scrambles backwards, rushing off to the counter as I sit there, head reeling with information. Gormliath is a small nation of islands off the Western shore, over seven hundred miles from my birthplace, six kingdoms away. Everyone knows about this country; or at least, everyone knows the stories.

More than two decades ago, the king's wife died in childbirth and for reasons unknown, he sealed off the kingdom to any and all travelers, destroying all but one seaport and registering all its citizens. Armies from the emperor attempted to overpower the king and bring Gormliath back under the fold of the Great Empire, but the long, bitter winter proved too much for the soldiers from warm climates and Gormliath broke away, destroying the unity of the seven sacred kingdoms that made up the Great Empire. No one has set foot in Gormliath since that day, except to deliver goods and receive exports - but no outsider could enter the gates of the kingdom itself.

My head flicks up, scanning the room, searching for clues, and notice the tavern's staff whispering furtively in the corner, eyes trained on me. One of them nods, then rushes out the door.

This isn't good.

I wait until their backs are turned then slink down under the table and scurry behind the skirts of two passing patrons until I'm within arm's reach of the exit. Straightening into a nonchalant pose, I peer out the door, avoiding the warm orange glow from the lantern hanging above. I spot the barmaid waving down some guards, and with their attention on her I dart out the door. Keeping to the shadows, I sneak into an alley nearby.

I can't tell if it's my nerves or the heat of the sun-warmed stones against my back that are encouraging perspiration from my skin, but I still my breathing as much as possible and listen to the sounds at the entrance to the tavern.

"You said there's a woman inside, dressed like a man, who is a foreigner?"

"Yes. In the northwest corner." Their voices echo off the cobblestone streets, and my anxiety grows, wondering just how many others can hear the conversation as clearly as I can. Notoriety is only good for a thief when she herself controls it.

I hear the door swing open, and with a deep breath, I peek around the corner, watching the guards and barmaid step inside. The second the door shuts behind them, I race out into the street.

My eyes dart along the ground, up and down each side of the long high street, finally spotting an old woman crouched against a building. Her hair is matted, pushed over to one side, and her clothes are torn and dirty. She beckons me closer, urgently waving me in.

She looks oddly familiar and I hesitate, calculating my chances of instead navigating an unfamiliar city late at night with no weapon. Deciding I'd rather risk it with an old woman, I slide in next to her and duck my head down, peering up at her from beneath my lashes.

I don't believe it! It's the woman from the roadside who helped me bandage my side just hours before. Alarmed, I look up at her in surprise. "What are you-?!"

She lifts an arm and thwacks me over the head. "Stupid! Sit still and shut your mouth!"

Hastily I tuck my head down to her side, grateful for the tatters and tears in my clothing. The woman's stench is intense, but I don't have time to dwell on it; two seconds more and I hold my breath at the sound of the guards bursting forth from the tavern, shouting to each other to spread out and search for me. One makes off quickly in the other direction, but one runs full speed towards us and I have to will myself to keep breathing from my huddled spot on the ground.

The guard rushes past, thrusting a lantern into the darkness down each alley. "Dammit!" He changes course to run down another nearby alleyway.

Once the coast is clear, I hear a laugh that can only be described as a cackle emerge from the woman's face above me. I untuck my head and sit up, looking at her amused expression.

"You're a wanted woman, I see."

"I am."

She clicks her tongue, smiling a toothless smile. "I could feed myself for a whole year with what I might get for turning you in."

"You could. But you won't." I return her smile.

"No?"

"Because you're a thief, and thieves have honor."

Her laugh this time is downright obscene, shrieking loud and high over the cobblestones. "That I am." She taps her forearm, the skin a rippled mess where the Empire's thieves' brand is seared into her skin. Her eyes flit to my own arm and I roll up my sleeve to show her the smooth and unscarred flesh.

"I've never been caught." My eyes sparkle and she claps her hands in delight.

"Come with me. Let's get you taken care of."

Pushing off the wall behind her, she rises nimbly onto a pair of surprisingly steady feet. I leap up to follow, admiration welling up in me at her movements. Apparently, old thief habits die hard.

We cut down narrow alleyways, avoiding well-lit streets. Everywhere I look, walls and fences are covered with papers of missing persons, some official and many handmade. They flutter in the quiet evening breeze giving an eerie feeling to the city. I try and make out their details, but they're all so... generic. Gone missing. Gone missing. Gone missing.

Eventually the woman stops before a sturdy oak door set into a long stone wall. She taps out a complex rhythm of knocks, and the door opens to a young man smiling at my companion. When his eyes alight on me, his face falls and his mouth sets into a firm line.

"Uma, who is this?"

"She's with me, and that's all you need to know." Uma shoulders past the man, firmly enough to send him back a step and I snicker, stepping through the doorframe and ducking my head to avoid the lintel. Standing at my full height once inside the room, I match him eye to eye and he swallows thickly.

"Don't just stand there, Andrew! Fetch some water for our guest!" Uma drops her cloak onto a nearby chair and scuttles over to a bed in the corner. Andrew sighs, and steps out of the room, leaving me to watch Uma. The lighting is dim, but my eyes adjust to the candlelight and I see that Uma is hovering over a girl laying in a bed.

Soft murmurs of affection tumble from Uma's lips, and she gently strokes the sweat-soaked forehead of the young woman.

Awkwardly, I wait for Uma to finish, my bruises and muscle aches catching up to me now that my adrenaline is running off. I fail to stifle a yawn, and Uma looks up at me, as if remembering I am still there.

"Is that dreaded boy not back yet?" Pushing her hair back she sighs, gesturing towards the girl on the bed. "This is Enora, Andrew's sister. Their parents lived here years ago, but when they died Andrew took to stealing in order to feed them. He wasn't very good, but I've managed to teach him a few things." She winks at me, but the smile on her face fades quickly, looking back to the girl. "The little thing has fallen ill, and we don't seem to know how or why. No one else seems to have caught it. But she's just wasting away, and we've not got the money to hire a healer for her."

Uma backs away from the bed and turns to tend the fire, burning hotly even in the warm summer months. I take a step closer, observing the girls' sallow skin that stands in contrast to the pillow beneath her head. The second I bend down to get a closer look, I hear the scrape of metal and feel a sharp heat near the side of my face.

"Move just an inch, and I'll slide this into the back of your head, hear me?" The searing-hot iron of the fire poker hovers just below my ear.

Seriously? Again? Based on today alone, I'm concluding that Gormliath's hospitality is one for the ages.

Trying my best to feign a lack of concern, I roll my shoulders. "You know... I'm faster, younger, and stronger than you. Do you really think this will work out in your favor?"

"I'm no fool. But I've got your attention. And you're going to do what I say or I'll call the guards and tell them the foreigner broke into my home and threatened me."

"Then what would you have me do?"

"Heal her. Figure out what's wrong."

I grit my teeth, wishing I could see the woman's face. "You could have just asked."

She sets the poker down, satisfied, though I notice it stays within quick reach of her long bony fingers. Sighing to myself at my impressive misfortune, I look at the girl again. It's dark in this little corner of the room and I motion to the candle on a nearby table. "May I?"

Uma shrugs. "Do what you need to do."

Lifting the candle, I hold the light above the bed, pressing the back of my hand to Enora's forehead. Cold to the touch, her breathing is gentle but sweat beads upon her hairline.

"How long has she been like this?"

"Little over a week."

Bet you anything she's been bit by something, but venom from a bite doesn't usually last this long- one week in and you're either better, or dead... unless you're still being bitten.

"Have you bathed her? Checked for bite marks or strange patterns on the skin?"

"Yes, even just yesterday. She's got nothing on her." Frowning, Uma steps closer.

Gently, I place a hand on each side of Enora's head and slide my fingers along her scalp, under her hair.

The door opens and Andrew walks in, a skin of water in his arms. "What are you doing to her?" He shouts at me, tossing the parcel on the floor as he rushes towards his sister.

"Andrew!" Uma's shout is fierce and he halts his movement, half a stride from me, eyes bulging with rage. "She's helping. Leave her to it."

Andrew scowls at me but he doesn't move, and Uma makes a small, satisfied sound in the back of her throat.

Mentally noting the absolute authority that Uma has over the young man, I continue my work. Closing my eyes, I feel along the highest ridges of Enora's spine until my index finger makes contact with a small, squishy spot protruding from the skin. "Ah."

Uma looks at me, surprised. "What did you find?"

"I've got to turn her."

Andrew and Uma both step closer, watching intently. Sliding my arms beneath her, I roll the girl onto her side. "Here." Taking Uma's hand, I guide her fingers along the back of Enora's skull until I see Uma's eyes go wide.

"What is that?"

"A dragon wisp, most likely." Taking care not to disturb the leech-like insect, I gently pull her hair away from the spot, revealing the typical bright red spines that give the bug its name. "As I suspected."

"Would ya look at that?" Uma peers at the bulging red ball and Andrew moves in to get a closer look. "I looked for all sorts of beasties that might have bitten her. But I didn't think to check her hair."

"It's unlikely you would have found anything even if you had. They're small little creatures to begin with, growing as they fill with blood. Could have been half this size only yesterday."

"So what do we do about it?" Andrew's voice is quiet, and he stares at the creature with a mixture of curiosity and disgust. "And... how did she get that thing?"

I chew on my lips, thoughts coming up blank with my lack of information about the area I've found myself in. Hesitant to inform Uma and the others of that morsel of truth, I carefully piece together my words.

"I'm afraid I'm not exactly sure how to answer your second question. But to the first... I can help." I glance around the room, taking stock of what they have. I reach above my head and pull down a bunch of dried lavender hanging from the rafters. "Andrew, have you seen any myrtle sap being sold in the marketplace?"

His worn and dirty fingers touch his chin, attempting to play with the slight stubble of a beard that refuses to grow. "I think the old apothecary shop at the end of the row has some."

A sly smile settles onto my lips. "Care to go and flex your skills? Your sister will need some." He grins at me, eager to show off, and starts for the door. Mentally calculating the last ingredients, I shout after him. "Oh and grab some thistle bark while you are there!"

Waving his arms behind him in understanding, he disappears into the night, and I get to work. Uma watches with quiet fascination and a hint of skepticism as I lift a bowl down from a high shelf and set it on the small table. She hands me the mortar and pestle and I smash the lavender into a fine powder, then toss it into the bowl.

Realizing that I'm left without a knife after this afternoon's incident, I bite the inside of my cheek, brow furrowing in thought.

"What is it?" Uma leans in, studying my face.

"My knife... it, well, I lost it. Today."

"If you need one now, use one of these." Uma scurries across the room and takes a leather wrap from a low shelf, unrolling it before me. A fantastic selection of utility knives, lockpicks, and other tools are neatly bundled, individual sleeves protecting each blade. I grin and peer over each until I find one that should do just the trick for cutting out the insect.

A few minutes more and Andrew scurries in the door, breathing hard. "Catch!"

He tosses the bundle in the air and I grab it cleanly, unwrapping the cloth to find a neatly sealed bottle of myrtle sap and a few bunches of thistle bark tucked neatly inside.

Grinding the bark down, I toss the powdery brown substance into the bowl with the lavender, then carefully pour in half the bottle of the sticky green liquid.

Mashing a clove of garlic and a few sprinkles of salt, I add them to the bowl and mix as well as I can, the sap proving a sticky and difficult opponent. Once the sap is mixed well enough with the other ingredients, I set the bowl on top of a pot hanging over the fire, and let it get warm. When the sap is looser and more fluid, I turn to Uma and Andrew. "Ready?"

They nod in unison, and I can't help but smile at their familiarity. They may not be family, but I can tell they've been together for quite some time. No longer viewed with suspicion or as a threat, their faces are open and trusting, ready for my instructions. "I'm going to have to cut the insect out - it will take some of the flesh - but there's no way to remove them otherwise. Once the wisp is gone, spread this mixture on the back of her neck as quickly as possible, covering the whole area. It's going to burn. She's going to fight you, and scream, and it's going to hurt her. You must keep it going. This will cleanse the wound and kill the toxins. Do you understand?"

Solemn faces greet me, and I can see the distinctive glimmer of fear in Andrew's eyes, but determination and love win out; the two move to my side, ready to help.

Selecting my blade of choice, I move to Enora's bed and sit beside her. A few slow, steady breaths, and I flick my eyes open, pressing the knife into the girl's skin.

I cut quickly, moving to the ground so I can kneel and get a better vantage point. I can't go too deep for risk of hitting bone, but I must cut deep enough or the wisp's teeth will remain. With effort, I tug at her skin, trying to create impossible space between flesh and bone, hoping that she remains unharmed.

The fire in the room feels sweltering but I'm grateful for the light, and Uma holds the candle above my head for better vision. "Andrew, I'm about to make the last cut. Get ready."

The young man is sweating, but he nods rapidly, picking up the bowl and plunging his knife into the hot, sticky substance and coating the blade.

With a final flick of my wrist, my knife slides beneath the head of the insect and the wisp falls away to the floor. Stomping on the blood-filled creature until I am sure it is thoroughly dead, I scoop it up with a cloth and toss it into the fire.

Turning, I watch Andrew begin to spread the ointment on Enora's wound. The second it touches her skin, her eyes shoot open and she lets out a blood-curdling scream. Uma thrusts the candle onto the nearby table and grabs the girl's arms, holding them to her side, whispering in her ear. "You're all right, little mouse. You're all right."

Hands shaking, Andrew continues to cover the wound in the sap, mumbling what I can only assume are prayers to himself. Once the wound is covered, Enora's screaming turns to sobs, and she wails into Uma's skirts, Andrew sinking onto the floor, the bowl clattering at his feet.

Not wanting to intrude, I turn my eyes to the tips of my boots, until I hear Enora's cries soften. When she speaks, her voice is soft, hoarse from the crying. "Uma?"

"Yes, child?"

"I'm hungry."

A bark of laughter escapes Andrew's lips and he rises to his knees, kissing the top of his sister's head. "I'll go get you something to eat."

Standing, he walks to me and pauses, muttering "Thank you," before striding out of the house.

I watch as Uma strokes the girl's hair, then clear my throat. Uma's eyes find mine and she stares at me for a few seconds, before setting her lips into a thin line.

"Thank you for healing her."

I scoff, staring at the old woman. "It's not like I had a choice."

Eyes narrowing, Uma shakes her head. "You always have a choice."

I don't respond, and I hope she understands my skepticism.

Sighing, she bends and kisses the girl's forehead, then rises to meet me. "What is it that you want, then? How can I pay you for this?"

I lean against the doorframe, studying her. I know it's a risk, but she's the only one who suspects that I'm a foreigner and doesn't seem keen on turning me in to the authorities. Closing my eyes, I take a deep breath. "You can pay me with information. I need to know how I came to be in Gormliath."

3

The tense silence that greets me is enough to know that I've made a mistake. I should go, and quickly. I'm about to dart out the door when Enora sits up in the bed, squealing loudly. "This is so exciting! Uma, did you hear her? Did you hear? She's an outsider!" She tugs on the sleeve of the old woman, eyes crinkled in glee.

"I heard." Uma's voice is stone cold, eyes slowly taking me in. "And to think I wasn't sure it was true. How could it be? And yet here you are." The muscles in her arm flex and I grit my jaw, bracing myself for her next question. "Tell me, then. Where do you hail from?"

At that moment, Andrew steps back in through the door, a loaf of bread under one arm and a small parcel wrapped in cheesecloth in his hand. He looks between us, stepping into the tension, and his eyes narrow. "What's all this?"

Squaring his shoulders he attempts to fill the doorframe, a gesture I'd find far more humorous under other circumstances. But the hawk-like glare in Uma's eyes is no laughing matter, and Enora is torn between fear and curiosity, eyes widely fixated on me.

"Answer me. From where do you hail?" Uma's eyes flick over to Andrew for half a second and he relaxes a fraction but remains a solid block against my exit.

Calculating the predicament I find myself in, I realize that I must tell the truth. Uma could be a valuable ally and though I was forced into it, Enora sits bright eyed before her due to my actions. Trained well,

Uma's keen ability to read people is still active, and she'll know if I'm lying.

"I have lived a life on the road for almost twenty years now, but when I was born, it was in Nerogaia."

Uma's eyes flash, a mix of confusion and raw hope. Rushing towards me, she grabs the front of my vest. "This mother you spoke of. What was her name?"

"Why should I tell you?" Confused by her frantic actions, I shrug out of her grasp with a violent shrug.

"Was it Althaea? Was Althaea your mother's name?"

My eyes go wide, and I gasp in unadulterated shock. There is a desperate look etched into her features, and I nod ever so slightly in my bewilderment.

When she speaks, it is a whisper. "Althaea?" Moving as slow as honey on a winter's day, she lifts her hands and places them gingerly on the sides of my face. "You are... Althaea's girl?"

A sharp inhale of breath, and I stumble backwards. "You know my mother?"

Uma stares at me, eyes full of wonder. "Your mother was the most famous healer in the seven sacred kingdoms." Her long, crooked fingers trace the outline of my hands. "Your gift. It's part of you. You have her magic in you."

I press a hand to my chest, trying to master control of my suddenly unsteady breathing. The onslaught of new information overwhelms me. Does this explain mother's frequent trips away? Flashes of memories with my mother flood my brain but they soon settle on one distinct scene: mother and eight-year-old me, sitting along the rocky coast, wind whipping at our hair. She had told me then that she was leaving again. This time, she was leaving to do something that was difficult; something so hard that even she wasn't sure she could do it - but it was important... and she needed to try. She had said, "Sometimes, we have to do what we know is right, even when we know it is wrong." This confused me as a child, but she had often whispered enigmatic things to me while she was lost in her thoughts, so I had considered nothing unusual in her cryptic statement.

I smiled at her, she kissed my hair... and then mounted her jet-black stallion and rode away. I never saw her again.

I am snapped out of my thoughts by the touch of a small hand on my arm. Enora stands before me, a curious smile on her face. "Where is Nerogaia?"

Shaking the memory out of my head, I look down at her and force a smile to my lips. "It's on the other side of the world."

Her eyes light up with curiosity, and her lips part, ready with a barrage of questions for me, but Uma steps in and beckons to Andrew.

"Andrew - take your sister and go entertain yourselves."

"Are you sure it's safe? I don't want to leave you here with this... with her." While Uma and Enora have switched from hostile regard to my presence, Andrew is less convinced.

"She is no threat to me. Go. Have fun. Buy her a gift. Spoil our love a little. She's been through a lot tonight." Uma smiles, flipping a large silver coin out of her hand towards him. Andrew's eyes grow wide as he catches it cleanly.

"Uma, where did you get this?"

She grins wickedly, showing my coin purse in her palm. She tosses it back to me, winking at him. "She's treating you tonight."

"Fantastic." Smiling broadly, he grabs his sister's hand and darts out the door.

Uma lifts her chin, pointing at my coin purse. "Sorry about that, but you're not exactly hurting for silver these days, and it looked like you needed a minute."

A thick swallow tugs at the inside of my throat and I realize that I'm grateful for the time to process. "My mother... What do you know about her?"

Uma leads me gently to the bed and takes a seat beside me.

"I knew her well... though not for long. Met her one day on the side of a road near the port town that connected the kingdoms of Gormliath and Haverdale. Back then, I worked for the Queen of Haverdale as one of her informants in Gormliath. We may all have been part of the same empire, but hostility between kingdoms was always there, hiding beneath the surface. I was trying to outrun a group of bandits; I'd learned the leader was attempting to steal a sacred artifact, and I knew the mission would get me good information. I sold them a story that I was one of them, ready and eager to help. But, well.... I guess I'm a better thief than a theatre performer. They discovered my ruse and were hot on my trail when I stumbled and fell down into a ravine, breaking my leg in the process. Your mother was racing along on her horse, but she stopped when she saw me. She pulled me out of the water, helped me onto her horse, and promised she'd tend me later. We rode for another hour, deep into the mountains until we arrived at a makeshift camp, hidden away in an enclave hidden by gorse bushes. The pain on the journey was excruciating, but she saved my life that day. I stayed at her camp for a few months while she visited the ailing and aching all over Gormliath." Uma draws in a deep breath, her eyes distant in memory. "Your mother was always kind. She had the softest smile, though she was a warrior at heart. I've never met a woman so brave. Nothing phased her." Uma's eyes lift, focusing on me, and she tucks a loose strand of hair behind my ear. "You look just like her, you know that? You have the same fire in your eyes. I saw it yesterday, almost immediately, but dismissed it outright. Why would Althaea be here, again?"

Uma stands, gingerly rubbing a hand along her sore back. "All the same. She was a good friend to me. She helped me."

The brand on Uma's arm is visible, and I point to it. "How did you end up with that, then?"

She sighs, a complicated look on her face. "After the queen's death, the ports shut down and the borders closed. I was stuck here. With no way to reach Haverdale and return home, my money soon ran out, and I had to put my skills to good use. Thieving seemed a natural choice. I was caught once, years ago... served my time, and I've been begging on the streets, with a side of mischief, ever since."

I grin, understanding the way life pushed me into the same occupation.

She sighs and pats my hand. Mind still swimming, I realize I need time to process all of this. "Uma, is there a tree nearby, in a quiet spot?"

"A tree? Whatever for?"

"I need to sleep. And I don't want to be missing out on any more silver when I wake up." I smile wearily at her, and she returns it.

"Aye. There's a great chestnut tree just south of the city center. It's down a row of houses; it should be quiet now."

"Thank you."

Turning to go, I pause when I hear her speak softly behind me. "You should know... whatever answers you seek - the palace will be where you find them. It is the seat of all magic in Gormliath. There is an oak tree in the courtyard; its roots cover the ground the palace is built on, and it grows taller than the castle walls. There's not a corner in that place not affected by it. If you need to find your way home, the castle is where you should go." She smiles kindly, the way I imagine a grandmother would. "Now, go. Have your rest. Clear your head. Come back in the morning, and we'll see about mending your clothes for you. You healed my Enora. You are Althaea's daughter. You are always welcome here."

I consider her words and nod briefly, disappearing into the night.

*****

It's perfect. I spin a bit, looking down at the way it fits to my form. The skill at which the twelve-year-old has finished the dress is intriguing. Knowing her tiny hands made this is astounding. "Enora, it's exactly what I wanted. You're quite good at this."

Her cheeks stain crimson at the praise, and she looks down. "Thank you. You saved me, so I wanted to make it special."

Uma scuttles over, patting the girl's head gently. "Oh, hush. Enora's mother was a seamstress, and taught her well - now, she takes in mending jobs. Somebody here has to make an honest living." She winks at the girl, whose blush grows deeper.

"Well, it's lovely, and your work is fine." I brush my hands down the front of the skirt and over my hips, noticing small slits in the fabric. "What's this?"

Eyes sparkling, Enora approaches me. "I made a few small changes to a normal dress. I noticed that you had a knife holster under your arm, and another on your hip. I stitched in some places where you can grab them quickly if you want." She points down towards my boots, beaming. "The skirt has a few extra pleats in it, as well: to make it better for when you need to take longer strides or jump over something, and I hemmed it a few inches shorter so you can run easily without having to hold it up."

Looking down, I can see the sides of my boots just visible beneath the hem. "You're brilliant, Enora!"

I'm afraid the girl is about to burst from embarrassed pride, but Uma smiles and changes the subject.

"There's one last thing for you before you go."

Rummaging under the bed, she pulls a small cedar box into view. As she opens it, I peer over her shoulder and see what must be the total of all possessions of value; a small silver mirror, a fine feather quill, a few old coins, and a leather-bound book. Uma lifts the book, and from beneath it withdraws a beautiful dagger. A stunning garnet set into a bronze-cast hilt that meets steel of fine craftsmanship, honed to a brilliant point.

"This was a gift from my queen. I have kept it all these years, but now it is yours. Your mother would want you to have this to protect yourself. I hope it brings you luck."

She shuffles closer, setting the blade in my palm, and gently closes my fingers around it.

"I don't know why you are here... or what your purpose is... but I believe all great mysteries are worth solving."

An unfamiliar stinging sensation pricks at the corner of my eyes, and I bow my head to her, kissing the back of her grizzled old hand.

"Thank you."

The door opens and Andrew walks in, basket looped over one of his arms. He clears his throat awkwardly but thrusts the basket into my arms.

"Bread... for... you know... eating. And some meat. And a skin of water."

"For drinking?" I tease.

He coughs out an agreement and spins on his heel, leaving as quickly as he came in.

Uma's warm chuckle lifts over my shoulder, and I catch a glimpse of Enora shaking her head in amused disbelief at her older brother. "He'll never catch a wife like that."

Giggling, I collect my gifts and belongings. Enora hands me one last stack of clothes - my mended clothing from before - and I look to the two of them.

"Truly, I cannot thank you enough. I am honored." I slide the dagger into the harness on my side and tuck the rest of my new belongings under my arm.

"I'll walk you outside. Say goodbye, Enora." Uma pushes Enora towards me and she leaps into my arms, pressing her cheek to my chest. "I'll miss you."

Laughing, I extricate myself from her arms. "And I'll miss you." I tap the end of her nose, then tuck a stray hair behind her ear. "You're a strong girl, and you've got a good life ahead of you now. Thank you for the clothes. I'll be forever grateful."

"You're welcome!"

The sun is high in the sky by the time I step outside, and when my eyes adjust to the light, I see a somewhat pained expression on Uma's face.

"What is it?"

Her eyes are steady but she lets out a deep sigh. "Before you set out, there is one thing you must know." The heaviness in her voice gives me pause.

"Tell me."

"It's about your mother. Be careful, in the palace. Do not let the king see you. You look so much like your mother..."

Her voice trails off, and I urge her to continue. "Uma... what are you trying to tell me?"

When she speaks, her eyes are wild, and the words she utters cripple me with fear.

"Althaea... She... She was the one with the ailing queen just before her death. She is the one King Alexander blamed the queen's death on, and the reason Gormliath closed its borders. Your mother is said to be the one who cursed the queen and sent her to her death."

4

"That's a lie!" The first words out of my mouth are urgent and fearful but the somber stare I receive from Uma assures me that she speaks the truth.

"My mother killed her?"

A withered hand lands softly on my arm, squeezing reassuringly. "It is the rumor. Your mother was a great healer, we know. And the queen was not the first nor the last woman to die in childbirth. But something about her visit that day turned the King's heart to ice. Your mother went on the run. I never knew what happened to her, except that the King demanded her head, and broadcast her image all over the kingdom. I wondered if she had found a way to escape and live a happy life. I suppose that was naive, but we never learned of her capture so I've always held onto hope."

"This was twenty-two years ago?"

Uma nods, watching as my mental calculations all come to place.

"She never came home. I was only eight." An unknown anger bubbles up inside of me and I find myself raising my voice. "How could she? How could she leave and never come back, to embroil herself in these schemes, to change my life forever? I was just a little girl!"

"Hush, my friend!" Uma grabs my arms to stop my pacing. "Neither of us know the truth, but your mother was a good woman. Trust in her. Trust in yourself. I pray you will find the answers to this and more, but you cannot begin your journey with rage as a motive. Calm your heart.

She was good, and she loved you. Believe in what you know. Let your memories guide you."

Calming slightly, I close my eyes and repeat the words in my head. *Believe in what you know. Let your memories guide you.* Though sadness and pain threaten to overtake me, Uma is correct. I must be strong. I have no idea why I'm here or what I'm doing, but I'll figure it out

"You're right. I'm sorry."

A warm, low chuckle rumbles from deep within the frail woman's chest. "Don't you fret. We all have our burdens. Though, it is a good thing you are so strong." She winks at me and taps my hand.

I look to Uma, wondering. She's not young, and while she has Andrew and Enora to care for her, I wonder just how many more summer sunrises she may live to see.

"What will you do next?"

"Ahhh... I imagine I will walk to the temple of Camilla and light a candle for your mother. And then, well... I'll enjoy an old woman's life."

She pauses for a minute, then smiles. "Now go. Shoo. And may the goddess guide you."

With a nod of approval and a wink at Uma, I set out into the early morning sunshine.

*****

Gently sliding my fingers against the cool stone, I close my eyes, concentrating on the texture beneath my fingertips. It should be just here... Eyes flying open when at last I can feel the smooth cowhide, I twist in place and rise to the tops of my toes, trying to peer in through the window. Tugging the makeshift curtain a fraction of an inch to the left, I cup my other hand around my eyes, trying to adjust to the darkness within the old stable. Once things come into focus, I can see him; the great beast known as Curaidh.

This is the place.

I drop down to my feet, take a deep breath, and square my shoulders. Wait. No. This isn't right. Silently cursing the fact that my parents never even attempted to instill a lady's education on me, I think of the way I have seen more typical women carry themselves. My first thought goes to the haughty and dismissive women who attended the princess on the road; but no, I am to play no court lady. Instead, I fashion my behaviors and stance after the women I'd seen perusing goods in the market. I wiggle my arms a bit, trying to adopt a more free-flowing style to my movements. Feeling satisfied enough, I round the corner with my basket of flowers and enter the stable.

A large man with ill-fitting clothes held on only by the worn belt around his waist is bent over a large tub of water, filling smaller buckets. A young boy with red hair and skin covered in freckles is asleep in the hay further into the stable. Assuming the gentleman is employed here, I approach him.

"Good day to you, sir. I am looking for the stable master."

In comical fashion, the man rises with a start, smacking his head on a saddle bar above and sloshing water all over his boots. His cry of pain startles the young boy awake, who jolts awake, bewildered and wide eyed, a piece of wayward straw stuck in his hair, sticking sideways out of the side of his head. I almost let out a whoop of laughter, but remembering my attempt at femininity, I move forward, anxiety for his condition plain in my expression. "Forgive me! It was not my intent to startle you."

Bending down, I peer into the man's eyes as they fill with tears from the injury. "Are you alright?"

He nods his head at me, squinting through the pain. "Aye, aye I'm alright. Give me a mo', would ya?"

I scurry backwards, a look of polite concern on my face. "Of course, sir. My apologies."

The large man rises, touching his fingers to his head, testing it out. Seeing no blood upon inspection, he shakes his head roughly and splashes water on his face. Observing him to be a bit of a wild man, I fight the smile on my face.

Stealing a glance at the young boy, I notice his eyes darting back and forth between the two of us. Offering him a gentle smile, his eyes drop to the floor.

Satisfied with his condition at last, the man turns to me. "Who are you?"

His voice is cross, and thick black eyebrows furrow down his brow as he glares at me.

"Forgive me for the intrusion, good sir. As I said, I'm looking for the stable master."

Roughly rubbing his face with an old piece of cloth hanging from a nearby hook, he stares me down, new smudges left behind on his sun-withered skin. "Well, you've found 'im. What're you doing here?" There is an air of suspicion to his voice, and his eyes are piercing. I cock my head, smile sweetly, and look down at the bundle in my arms.

"I was passing by and merely wished to come and bring this apple to Curaidh." Rummaging into the basket of flowers, I proudly display a juicy pink apple in my palm.

The man's eyes narrow even more as he inspects the fruit in my hand and the boy visibly licks his lips, moving forward a fraction.

"You'd offer that fruit to a horse?"

"I would. But, if you're hungry... I have more." Pulling back the cloth covering the remaining contents of my basket, I show a dozen apples, freshly purchased from the market that day. It cost me two whole pieces of silver to buy this many, but bribery does wonders and I considered it a worthwhile investment.

Grinning, I toss one at the boy who scrambles across the hay, snatching it greedily and plunging his teeth through the skin and into the juicy bits. Obscene noises come from his lips as he devours the fruit.

"Ewan! You're not an animal. Don't behave like one." The man scowls at the boy, who gulps down a massive mouthful and nods solemnly.

"Forgive us for that unfit display," the man forces himself to say, slowly bringing his eyes back to mine.

"Not at all. Now... about the horse..." I hand the man an apple and move past him, trying to remember not to step too heavily. Approaching Curaidh, I smile.

"Hello, sweet boy. Feeling better, are we?"

I reach over, arm outstretched, and he moves to me, pressing his nose to my palm. "There we are."

Dipping my hand into my basket, I pull an apple out and lay it flat in my hand. "Here you go, boy."

The majestic stallion bends his head and plucks it out of my palm in one quick motion, chomping it to bits, snuffling around in the hay at his feet to clean up any lost morsels. Giggling, I rub his neck and scratch behind his ears, slowly making my way around to his side.

The man sets down his apple, less willing to let my presence slide than I had hoped. He takes a slow step closer to me and I notice one hand move towards the side of his hip, then twitch and go limp. I know that movement well, having done it myself many times: reaching for my weapon on instinct before remembering where I am and who I am with. *Interesting.*

His fingers curl around themselves before settling on his belt, and he points at me with his chin. "What do you think you're doing then, eh?"

"This horse had an injury not long ago. I'm hoping to see how he is progressing." Careful to keep the details to a minimum and knowing that the stable's staff members might have somehow been involved in the horse's injury in the first place, I carefully observe the man's behavior and facial expressions while pretending to look at the horse.

"How'd you know that?"

So simple-minded and cross is his demeanor, I have to keep myself from rolling my eyes. "I was there."

Bending down to pick up Curaidh's foot, I peek at the underside, satisfied with the improvement. Dropping his hoof, I ruffle the hair on his neck. "Good lad, Curaidh! You're doing quite well."

I can tell the man is watching me, silently scrutinizing through his curmudgeonly attitude. Taking on an air of absolute nonchalance, I continue to coo at the horse, wooing his affections.

Finally, the gruff voice speaks behind me. "Last person touched him like that got kicked right square in the chest. Died two days ago." He nods his head at Curaidh. "Always been a good horse, but he'll let not a soul touch him this past week, and the princess hasn't even come down here since they returned. She used to ride every day but she's scared of him now. I think he's gone sour, and she knows it. He should've been left to die on that roadside. Whoever was that fixed him up was a fool."

My eyebrow lifts with amusement and I tilt my head to gaze upon his scrunched-up face. "Is that so?" I try to sound casual, not letting my face show the thoughts that run through my head. "He doesn't seem to mind me, much, now does he?" The man stares at me, a calculating expression on his face. The boy regards me with curiosity, almost as if he is unsure whether to be afraid or in awe.

"What's your name, then?"

"What's yours?"

He grunts out a sardonic laugh. "Sam." Hiking a finger over his shoulder, he gestures to the boy. "An' that's Ewan. He don't talk."

I nod to Sam and offer a small curtsy to Ewan. "It's lovely to meet you."

Cheeks burning suddenly bright, the boy tucks himself behind Sam's broad frame and I laugh lightly.

"This person who died... what was his role here?"

Sam scrutinizes me carefully. "The one got himself kicked to death? Well, he was the groom for that horse. Knew him well. That's how we all could tell something had changed about him."

Adopting an innocent smile, I stroke Curaidh's nose again. "If you need a replacement, I'd be happy to accept employment with you. It would be a gift to care for this noble creature."

Sam tilts his head, frowning. "You showing up here, it's awfully convenient-like."

"Don't you believe in luck, Sam?" I toss him a sly smile, and with a final kiss to the end of Curaidh's nose, I grab a broom from the wall and begin to sweep the horse's stall out, whistling quietly to myself.

Sam's voice calls out to me, a dark amusement in his tone. "I think it's a death wish, but alright, you can take the job if the princess allows it. She gets the final say. I can't just let you wander in and take over."

"Then why don't you go and seek her approval now? I'm eager to get to work. Let her know I'm here. I shall wait for her to arrive." I return to the sweeping and Sam snorts.

"As if a princess would come at your beck and call. Who do you think you are?"

Pausing, I turn to face the lumpy man and lean one hand on the end of the broom handle. "Tell her the girl with no name is applying for the position."

Sam's face is skeptical and a little wary, but all the same he shouts at Ewan to keep an eye on me, and he strides out the stable door.

I turn my eyes to Ewan, standing with his back against the wall opposite me, eyes a mixture of fascination and fear. "I won't bite, you know."

The corners of his lips tip downward into an infinitesimal frown, and I smile. "You can have another apple, if you'd like one. Just grab one from the basket there. I won't tell Sam."

Two blinks, with a full count between, and the boy lunges for the basket, grabbing another apple.

"What's this, then?" I ask him. "Have you eaten recently?" My brow furrows at the thought of a stable boy employed at the castle not being paid enough to at least eat a few meals per day.

He nods his head 'yes' at me, and I purse my lips. Suddenly, the thought comes to me, and I laugh. Fruits are hard to come by in Gormliath, and I suppose apples are even more so, based on the exorbitant price I paid at the market earlier that day. They're probably the equivalent to a delicious cocoa crème tart or a raspberry roll cake, two sweets a common townsperson could never hope to see, let alone eat. "Do you just love apples that much, then?"

He nods furiously, little red head bobbing up and down with the speed of an excited little bird.

"Well, I'll bring you another one again. I love them too."

The grin that meets me is wide, toothless, and enthusiastic. I giggle, then turn back to cleaning up the stall, mucking up the mess and pausing every few minutes to remind Curaidh that I'm still there, scratching his neck, and pulling bugs out of his mane.

Once satisfied, I grab a brush, and begin to smooth his coat, when I hear the rapidly approaching footsteps. Smirking, I know I'm in.

She bursts through the door, dark hair flying behind her, hands holding folds of her skirt so high they're clutched to her bosom.

"You!"

I curtsy, keeping my head low. "Yes, your highness?" My voice is demure, quiet, and I barely see Sam come rushing in behind the princess, breath heaving and face streaming perspiration.

My presentation makes her hesitate - I can tell suddenly she is unsure. Having not been granted permission to lift my head, I remain, eyes lowered, and hear her stutter a few times before finally getting her next sentence out.

"What is your name?"

I grin but drop my head even lower to hide my smile. "I'm afraid I cannot tell you that."

"It is you!" Her skirts drop in a heavy rustle and I realize she has let them down in her relief. "What are you doing here? And why are you dressed like that? I thought you said-"

I lift my head and stand tall, assuming the formalities are over with. "-that dresses are impossible infernos that one cannot work in?"

"Well, yes."

"I still hold that to be true. But one must admit that typically in polite company a woman wears a dress. I cannot present as the lawless ruffian that I am and hold employment, can I?"

She giggles, but a loud cough from Sam startles her and her eyes fly open then dart around as if realizing she is in the stables. Clearing her throat, she moves to her horse, who seems impatient to see her. Hesitantly, she reaches out her hand, biting her lower lip and looking like a small child touching a snake on a dare. The horse moves forward and she shrinks back, but instead of acting roughly, he tucks his face into her palm and closes his large brown eyes.

Her posture relaxes and she lets out a long wispy breath of relief. "There you are, love. There you are, my brave boy." She pets the side of his face, and I can see how much he loves her. She pushes her cheek against his and whispers quietly to him. "I'm sorry I haven't come to see you. I've missed you. Forgive me."

I shift in my stance, looking away, but I'm unable to hide the smile on my face. *'Forgive me', she asked her horse. What a charming creature she is.*

Sucking in a breath, the princess pulls back from her horse. After a minute, she speaks. "I am in need of a new groom. Why should I trust Curaidh to your care?" The same scrutinizing and critical glare from the roadside is on her face now and she attempts to level her eyes to mine, though she is at least five inches shorter than I am and I force myself not to smile at her vain attempt.

"Your horse trusts me, and I do quick work. I'm quiet and clean-"

The princess snorts, and realizing her error, covers it with a cough. "Please. Continue."

My upper lip twitches, threatening laughter, but I recover my composure. "Of course, your highness. As I was saying, along with being an employee that never gets in your way, I'll always have your horse ready for you, whether you need your carriage or wish to go for a quiet ride alone." I lower my voice and take a step towards her so that only the two of us can hear my next comments. "Forgive me, princess, but you haven't come to see your horse since the incident by the roadside. What happened? Are you frightened?"

Her eyes waver and she bites her lip, and for a moment I'm afraid I've pushed her too far but she lifts her head again, defiance creeping into her eyes. "You have one week to prove yourself." She turns to go but stops at the doorway. "I don't imagine that you will have any difficulty with this, but everyone who works in this stable is a man. There are grooms for all of my sisters' horses, my father's horses, and all the rest. It's a busy place and a big place, and there are many places where a woman might be caught unaware." She looks back at me, adding firmly, "Just... be careful."

Without waiting for an answer, she walks out.

5

The concerns of the princess are largely unfounded. I'm three days into my employment here and for the most part I've kept my head down. Up to this point, it's been a positive strategy; I act the unobtrusive woman, staying in my place and bothering no one while rumors swirl about me as people question who I am, where I'm from, and how I found favor with the princess so quickly. I haven't seen her yet, but that's another story.

I play the part of the obedient servant well... but what everyone around me doesn't know is that while I'm playing the part of a simple woman who follows the rules, I'm listening.

I listen to everything. Every morsel of gossip, every whisper between the chamber maids who come to flirt with the grooms, every insult slung to one another behind turned backs. I learned early on; it's amazing what someone will say when they think no one is listening.

However, as with all good things, my season of anonymity seems to have come to an end.

Two seconds ago, I was gathering tools to clean Curaidh's hooves. Now, a large burly fellow who works with the draft horses is behind me, my back pinned to his chest, a weak erection pushing against my buttocks as his fingers crawl across my bosom. His breath is almost more offensive than the attempt he is making at molesting me; it has clearly been a long time since he's had any such encounters, even of a consensual sort.

As the half-second of shock passes, I ram my elbow deep into his gut and stomp on his foot, turning around and smashing the palm of my hand upwards into his nose.

Howling, he runs out of the room shouting, "That bitch!" while I readjust my clothing and grab some nearby evergreen boughs, inhaling deeply in an attempt to snuff out the lingering stench he has left behind.

Ugh. I can taste it.

Spitting violently, I take a deep breath and rise to my full height, well aware that by this point I probably have some spectators. Turning around, I see four men and one of the palace maids, all looking scandalized; no doubt less by his actions, and more by mine.

"Well, well," I taunt them. "What a fine-looking group we have here. Come to catch the afternoon show?"

I begin to stalk towards them, and the maid squeaks and ducks behind one of the men, who all visibly shrink back as I approach.

"Anyone else interested?" I gesture lewdly to myself, and I'm met with a few gasps and one prayer at my indecency. Finally, one of them makes a sour face and motions for his fellow observers to walk away with him, their whispers making no attempt to hide their shock - and in some cases fear - at my self-defense.

Rolling my eyes, I brush some dirt off my dress, and return to my work.

A few minutes later, Sam comes rushing into Curaidh's stall, and a massive sigh of relief tumbles from his lips when he sees me calmly perched on my stool, cleaning the horse's hooves.

"You alright?" he grunts, looking even more annoyed than I do.

"Aside from feeling as if I need to scour my skin in boiling water and wash with juniper berries? Yes." Setting down Curaidh's hoof, I look up at Sam, keeping one hand on the horse's side to ensure he remembers I'm here. "Who was that?"

"He's no longer employed here, that's what."

My head snaps up at this; that doesn't make sense. "Did he quit?"

Sam's gaze is perfectly neutral. "No, I kicked him out. Can't very much have the princess' favorite getting felt up here, can I?"

I narrow my eyes at him, sure there is more.

"That, and he's a gorilla who spent more time lazing under the trees catching naps than doing any actual work. Finally had a reason to give him the boot."

"I see. Well, for what it's worth, thank you. I handled it, but I don't appreciate the unnecessary strain on my muscles. It's hard enough keeping this boy in check." I slap the broad chest of the great brown beast, and he tosses his head as if he agrees with me.

Sam hides a chuckle in his hand but tips his chin up to me. "Alright, then. That's that. Keep up the ... work."

I laugh at his intentional skipping of a compliment. "That I will."

*****

That afternoon, the princess finally makes an appearance. I barely hear her enter, soft slippers on the straw making nearly no sound. It's the subtle flash of sunlight glinting off her jewels that catches my eye, and I turn to look at her.

"Good afternoon, your highness." I dip my head in her direction, eyes following her as she barely pays me any attention. Her eyes are on her horse, traveling up and down his form.

"He looks well."

"Thank you." She still won't make eye contact with me but nods her head at my words.

Sighing, she looks down at her feet. "I heard about what happened to you. I'm glad you're alright."

Setting down the brush, I dust my hands off on the folds of my skirt. "I know you warned me of it but trust me. I can quite handle myself." She continues to stare at the ground, but I can see her jaw tighten so I continue. "I appreciate your concern all the same."

Finally looking up, her eyes are narrow and she seems to stare straight at me. "How are you so brave? And how are you so..." She pauses, waving her hands frantically in the air as she searches for the right word. "You?" Her finish is hilarious and I guffaw, but she continues, her brow furrowed so deeply that I can barely see her eyes any longer. "That man was nearly twice the size of you and you just ended it so easily!"

When she finally meets my gaze, her eyes are both hopeful and full of fearsome wonder. I shrug, years of apathy sourcing my response. "It's almost all I've ever known. I've been on my own since I was eight. I knew if I were to survive, I'd have to outlast everyone. First it was speed and keeping hidden, then it was strength and learning how to fight in a smart way."

The princess' eyes are wide and full of worry; the way they look when someone's about to say something dripping with pity for my existence. Not wanting to cut her off rudely, I lift a hand into the air and lay it flatly upon the top of my head. "Didn't hurt that I grew nice and tall, now, did it?" I wink at her, and her expression melts into a nervous smile, but I can tell I've altered her response.

"Ah, yes. I suppose you are rather large." She mumbles the words out then claps both hands over her lips, eyes wide in horror. I burst out in laughter, leaning against the rough stone wall as I clutch my sides. Her shoulders heave up and down, eyes darting to and fro as she searches desperately for a fitting apology, mouth flapping open and closed in staccato bursts of sound. "I! - Um! - Wha-!"

Having never seen the princess so out of sorts and embarrassed, I hold up my hand. "Please..." I punch out the words through my hiccups of laughter. "Don't apologize. That was refreshingly honest."

She scowls a bit at me, still clearly bewildered but now also confused as to my reaction. I hoot loudly, brushing the hair back from my face and beam at her. "You are a delight."

Clearing my throat, I close my eyes briefly to master my amusement and with a lingering smile on my face, address her directly. "Much as I appreciate your concern, your highness, I have a feeling it isn't the only reason for your visit to the stables this afternoon. So - would you care to tell me why you've come all this way?"

Still frowning at me, the princess's eyes slowly travel to the horse. "I thought I might go for a ride today."

"Oh! Excellent, yes." It's only now that I realize the princess is wearing a woolen riding cloak and a simple dress; hardly the attire of a well-adorned princess out for an afternoon stroll with her ladies in waiting. The jewelry resting across her collarbone, and the ribbon woven into her hair give away her status, but I can't help and appreciate the fact that this woman has an air of practicality to her.

"I'll ready Curaidh for you now, your highness."

"Wait!" She steps forward, reaching out her hand. "I'd..." Trailing off, she seems unsure, but it only lasts a split second. Shaking her head lightly, she purses her lips and begins again, a cold shift in formality to her demeanor. "I require a companion for my ride. Please ready my horse and prepare one for yourself as well."

With that, she spins and practically flees for the exit.

*****

As I step outside with Curaidh, I find the princess sitting by herself, fingers twisting over and over again in her lap. She spots us quickly and rises to her feet.

The groom I'd enlisted to help waits patiently while I hand off Curaidh's reins to the princess, then passes me the mare I've chosen for a ride. Named 'Morningsong', she's much smaller than Curaidh's frame, but she's strong and agile and didn't mind when I ran my fingers across her, other than to curiously try and inspect me while I said hello.

"Hello, darling," I coo at the horse, stroking her nose.

A prickly feeling shivers across the back of my neck, and I look over at the princess. She's fiddling with Curaidh's saddle though, and not paying me a bit of attention. Shifting my head slightly, I slowly move and look around, trying to see. Why do I feel like I'm being watched? Nothing looks amiss, anywhere. Every person I see is head-down, focused on their work, but the uneasy feeling doesn't go away.

A flurry of movement then catches my eye, and the princess is seated on her horse in one elegant movement. She peers down at me, a haughty look in her eyes. "Aren't you coming?"

Forgetting my distraction, I grin at the challenge in her voice and mount the horse quickly. "I think, your highness, that the question is.... Are you?" I click my tongue and squeeze my heels into the horse and we take off at lightning speed. I turn my head as I fly past her, just long enough to catch the look of shock on her face morph into a competitive scowl, eyes furrowed and mouth pressed into a thin-set line.

With a shout at Curaidh, they lurch forward, racing after Morningsong and me. I let out a gleeful whoop as we race along the path and out into the broad moors. For a quarter of an hour we ride, nothing between us but the journey.

Eventually the princess slows Curaidh to a walk and we fall in next to each other, slowly moving towards a creek running along the base of a mountain. Coming to a stop, she slides down from Curaidh's back, running a hand along his flank with a smile.

"It feels so good to be riding again." Her words seem to drift to no one in particular, but I hear them as I dismount and lead Morningsong to the water for a drink.

"Why did you stop?"

She pulls her cloak off, laying it softly into the grass and sits down, staring off into the distance. I plop into the dirt near her but maintain some separation. How close does one get to a princess in circumstances like this? I've no experience with royalty, but I'm not willing to alter my behavior to something socially acceptable unless I can get what I want out of her - and that is still to be decided.

The silence stretches on, and I take it that she won't be answering my question. So I flop backwards onto the earth, staring up into the crisp blue sky. A million wispy clouds dot the distant atmosphere like cotton tufts caught in brambles. The wind is still, and the clouds hover above me, barely moving.

"You're a good rider." The words catch my attention and I turn my head to look at her. Cheeks flushed from the exertion of the ride, stray hairs laying across her face, she looks vibrant and content. She smiles at me, somewhat shyly. "You're a good fighter too."

"I survive," I mutter dryly.

"Can you teach me?"

The question catches me off balance and I audibly stutter. "Teach you?"

"To fight." Her eyes are steel, boring holes into me. "I want to learn how to fight."

Staring at her, I can tell she's serious. "No."

"And why not?" She steps towards me firmly, hands on her hips.

The authenticity of her request concerns me, and I know that whatever this is, I don't want to get involved. "Thinking of pursuing a career in combat, are we?" Teasing is often a surefire way to escape commitment to, well, anything; but much to my weary resignation, the princess isn't quite so easy to fool.

"I'm completely serious. Teach me to fight."

"I won't -" she opens her mouth to retort, eyes blazing with fury but I hold up my hand and cut her off. "I won't teach you to fight, but I will teach you one trick. To defend yourself."

Her nose wrinkles and she purses her lips, but finally she huffs out a breath. "Will it keep me safe?"

"In some ways."

Her eyes travel up the length of my frame, sizing me up. "Can I do it?"

I laugh, my irritation melting away. "I guarantee that by the end of this, you'll be able to make *me* cry."

She practically squeals and leaps to her feet, standing at attention like a soldier in her father's army. I snort in amusement, rising to face her directly. Reaching out, I move to place my hands on her shoulders but stop, just short of touching her. I had not considered what sort of protocols there are with physical contact of a princess in an unknown land. Clearing my throat awkwardly, I look down. "May I?"

She either senses none of my discomfort, or I've massively underestimated her acting skills. Her tone is firm and focused. "Yes."

"Okay. Well." I rest my hands on her shoulders and let their weight settle there. "Relax."

I step back and she nods solemnly, bobbing her head up and down in a rapid movement.

"People are automatically going to assume that because you're a princess you'll have guards and be defenseless on your own. This move isn't a guarantee; not at all. But it can help."

A long blade of willow grass reaches to the heavens with its strong stalk, and I bend down and pluck it from the ground, spinning it between my fingers. "Our practice knife."

Stepping behind her, I awkwardly wrap my arms around her tiny frame, fighting a thousand voices in my head as they make jokes and obsess over whether I'll be executed for this later; but the princess is all business, so I squint my eyes shut tightly for two seconds and refocus, tightening my grip.

"Ow!"

"No offense, your highness, but any attacker you might face will have zero mind for your personal comfort."

She pauses and reconsiders, then grumpily agrees. "Proceed."

Pressing my makeshift knife against the delicate skin of her neck, she giggles at the action. "Hush," I scold her. "Now, this is scary, but you have to trust me. Everyone expects you to fight against the weapon. Nobody is waiting for you to give in to it - and that's the ticket out of this." She stiffens temporarily in my arms and I rush forward, talking her through the steps. "Reach up and grab the base of my thumb. Get your finger just under it, between your neck and my hand. Yes, that's good. Now as quick as you can, pull it back so that my arm twists away from you." She tries, and I shake my head. "No, like this. You need to twist towards the tip of the blade, and... you're going to get cut. But cut is better than dead." I tug on my own arm so she can see the spiraling motion and she tries again, a stern look of concentration written onto her brows. "Ow!"

She squeals in excitement as I shake out my wrist. "I did it!"

"You did part of it."

Her face falls comically and I grin at her. "Again."

Stepping back into place, I show her how to continue to twist the arm, causing the knife to fall. "And then you lift up your foot and stomp down, hard, onto the top of your attacker's foot."

Her knee lifts to the sky and I scramble to stop her. "Not right now! I'd like to be able to walk."

Over and over, we practice the routine until we're both sweating and tired. She isn't strong or mighty, but she's determined and there's a fierce gleam in her eyes that gives me a sense of confidence in her abilities.

"That's enough for today."

She smiles brightly at me, flopping into the dirt in a very un-princess-like manner, and I sink down beside her, leaning back against the ground. "You're very enigmatic, you know." She cocks her head at me, scrutinizing eyes mismatched from the amused grin on her face. "Who are you?"

I roll onto my side, elbow in the dirt as I prop my head upon my palm. Twisting my lips, I mull the situation over in my head, and I can see her eyes follow the movement. An involuntary smirk ghosts over my mouth, and she notices the shift, wide eyes flying up to meet my own.

"I am but a simple thief, your highness."

"I don't quite believe that is the whole story."

I pause, looking into her eyes. She holds my gaze firmly, any lingering fluster only a memory. "It isn't."

A look of uncertainty flashes in her eyes, but she doesn't act on it. "And what is your name?"

I laugh loudly at this. "I'm afraid I cannot tell you this."

"Cannot? Or will not?" She narrows her eyes, suddenly becoming a fierce shade of her bubbly self.

I pause, mulling it over. "Will not."

"Then I shall command you to tell me."

"Shall?" I snort, tracing circles in the ground beside me. "I highly doubt that you will."

"Whyever not? You sit... well, lie down before me so casually. You care for my horse. You are employed by my father. And yet you won't even tell me your name! I could have you killed for such a treasonous reply!"

"My dear princess, you'd never have the stomach for it. My name is but my last defense. I guard it well."

She glares at me, a fire in her eyes failing to disguise her internal struggle. She knows I'm right. The last in a long line of succession, she barely has any understanding of court politics and any power she has is mostly ceremonious, seriously limited by her father. Taking pity on her, I sigh a little. "I'm no one important. But on my honor as a thief, I'll never abuse your trust in me."

Sensing the hesitant truce between us, she chews on her lower lip. "And why should I believe you?"

"Because I like having friends in high places."

I roll once more onto my back, effectively ending the conversation. I can hear her huff out a breath of frustration, but then the noise shifts to a rustle of fabric and I peek over at her from the corner of my eye. She lays on her back, staring at the clouds like me, and I can't help but chuckle.

"I hardly imagine this a fitting display from a princess."

"That's none of your concern." Her voice is cross, a bit ill-tempered, and I can imagine the familiar scowl on her face. "Besides, if I am to figure out who you really are, we will become friends. And so you must stop calling me 'your highness.'"
A bark of laughter escapes my lips, and I grin at her. "And what shall I call you then?"

There's a long pause and I turn to look at her, only to see her opening and closing her mouth with a look of concentration on her face.

"I suppose I'm not sure. But many people call me Princess Meg. So that should do nicely."

"I see. Well, if that is your wish, Princess Meg, then that is what I shall call you."

"It's not like you're anything special at all, it's just that hearing you call me 'your highness' is so–"

I sit up suddenly, eyes darting about. That same feeling is back; an unsettling tickle on the back of one's neck when being watched.

"Quiet." I murmur.

"Excuse me?" She raises her voice, continuing. "Clearly, you misunderstand me! I am -"

I cut her off once more, raising a finger to my lips and shooting her a stern glare.

"Quiet!" I hiss at her under my breath, teeth bared. I lower myself, flat against the ground, eyes darting along the horizon, into the nearby trees, and all around me. There is no one... and yet, I know someone is nearby.

"We need to get back to the castle."

Without asking for permission, I grab her hand and yank her upright, whistling the horses nearby.

"What are you doing? What's going on?"

"We have to leave, now!" I leap onto Morningsong and the princess follows suit. With a shout we set off, urging our horses along as we race back towards the safety of the stables.

The entire ride back, I can feel the tense set of my shoulders and legs, neck twisting with pain as I continue to scan our surroundings. The princess rides well, navigating rough passages with ease and never once breaking her perfect posture.

After what feels like hours, we arrive back at the stables, completely unharmed and as far as I can tell, unfollowed. What was that? What on earth?

I stomp down the long corridor, roughly pulling on the horse's reins and slapping her rear into the stall.

I know my instincts. Someone was there. Someone was watching. But I couldn't see them! I couldn't find them, somehow. Clamping my eyes shut, I visualize the setting, scanning the horizon, the trees, the hillside. I search my memory for a flash of color, a blur of movement, even an unnatural shape along the ground... when a voice pulls me from my head.

"Will you please explain what that was all about?"

I look up to see her face, eyes full of fury and confusion. She stands stiffly, posture impeccable with her hands gripped in front of her. "You frightened me!"

It's then I notice the way her lower lip trembles, and how her forehead's wrinkles are pronounced.

"Goddess, I'm sorry." I draw my hands down over my face, exhaling a deep breath. "I... felt something."

"You *felt* something?" Her voice rises in pitch, and more than a few faces turn towards us. I step forward, hands outstretched in an attempt to calm her but she shakes away, curls bouncing with the movement. "You're a horrible human! How dare you!"

"Listen to me, please!" I beg her, shouting now, knowing I must get through to her. "It was... someone was there, watching us. We weren't alone and I don't know where they were or how close to us they were but you've got to believe me, someone was there! Someone was there and they were hiding." I flail about, trying to get my point across, speaking so quickly I'm not sure I'm being clear. "A guard or a wanderer wouldn't hide and if someone's hiding, it never means something good, princess. It means they're watching you. So I'm sorry if I frightened you, but I was frightened too!"

I look up, wondering if I have made my point, but my frustration melts to concern. She stands there, white as a ghost, lips parted gently in shock.

"I... I believe you. Thank you for explaining so thoroughly. But now I must go." She gathers herself and rushes towards the exit, then halts suddenly. Turning around, she looks at me once more. "Thank you for returning me safely."

And with that, she disappears into the setting sun.

*****

"Why, oh why do women have to wear skirts?" I mumble this in frustration as I finish getting dressed, cold fingers attempting to piece together all of the parts to my attire. The river I have been bathing in is unnaturally cold even in summer, but I know that Gormliath's winters are brutal due to their northern climate and I can only guess that the river is a sign of what might be to come.

Finally, the last ties are tied and final buttons buttoned and I yank at the skirt to straighten it out. Raising my arms up and down, I test out my movement, stretching this way and that. I can feel the weight of the dagger Uma gifted to me under my arm. It feels secure. After losing my own knife in the roadside incident, I am eternally grateful to Uma and her unconventional hospitality.

The weight in the holster there is bolstering, but it makes me acutely aware of the missing dagger of my mother. Made of Avalonian metal, it withstood even the greatest impact, was immune to poisons, and could not be melted down.

My mother's dagger was always an extension of her; a piece of her just like her heart. White crystals, emeralds, and bloodstones were embedded in the hilt. As a child, I always thought they made the dagger pretty. One day, my mother told me that any knife's selected stones were a vital part of the weapon, not just decoration. She never told me why these three were in hers, and I'd always meant to ask. I never got the chance.

I've always worn this empty holster since the day I left my home; the last reminder of my long-gone family. I never want to forget everything that I have lost. I need to know what happened to her. I need to know the truth. Did she really murder the queen - the princess's own mother? Or was she framed, and the real evil goes unpunished? Am I the forgotten child of a hero, or of a criminal?

This brief foray into reminiscing leaves me with a furrowed brow and tight shoulders, my teeth grinding in anguish. I shake my head roughly, trying to ease my emotions. This isn't me. I am a survivor. I move forward. I don't regret. Rolling my neck from side to side, I take a deep breath and center myself once again.

The main part of me wants nothing more than to get home. But... what is home? I've slept these past five nights in an ash tree near the river on the southern side of the castle walls. I've been wandering alone on the road for nearly twenty years. I have made my life in thieving, a nickname in every kingdom. In Veriterre, they called me "Le Fantome". In Haverdale, I was "The Black Dagger." I snort at that one. How original they were. Guess they'll have to come up with a new name, now that my black dagger is gone. *If I ever get back there...*

Sighing, I look to the sky. Maybe my mother never died. Maybe she's here. Maybe I'll find her. Or maybe this is all a lost cause... But something tells me I won't stop looking.

A hawk swoops low across the horizon and I realize how high the sun is. "Shit!" Stuffing my personal belongings into my pack, I scramble up the river's bank and race down the street, grateful for the skirt Enora made me. Panting and with sweat streaming down my face, I'm sure I look a lunatic as I sprint around the corner towards the castle's stables.

Skidding to a stop at the last second to avoid looking as late as I am, I tidy myself a bit and rub the inside of my skirt over my face in an attempt to erase some of the more obvious perspiration. I tuck my hair behind my ears, plaster on a smile, and move to take the last few steps to the door.

"It's a curse, I tell ye!"

My feet pause, knowing the value of every bit of gossip, and this sounds like a very good bit indeed.

"Curses be damned; there hasn't been real magic here since the queen died."

"Then why do you think they're acting like this? It's bad enough that they're walking around like they're empty inside their heads! Why just yesterday, Princess Agnes went and fell asleep in the bath, and Princess Euphemia had to send for a healer after Princess Gennet fainted during breakfast!" The voice lowers conspiratorially, and I can almost hear the dramatic movements that accompany their pause. "And what's more, each morning when the princesses all wake, every last one of 'em's dancing slippers are worn bare!"

I can hear Sam snort in disbelief. "That's a load of horse's shit if I ever heard one."

The same shrill voice gasps in affront. "Swear on me mum's grave, that's the honest truth!"

"Aye, get on with ye. If that's the 'honest truth' you've got empty-headed princesses waking up any minute demanding you pick up their pots for the morning relief, now don't you?"

A brief smile lights up my face, but now I realize Sam's finished putting up with gossip in his realm, and he'll soon notice my absence. Thinking better of revealing myself as an eavesdropper, I gather my skirts once more and run along the stone wall to the pasture, hoisting myself up and over just in time to grab an armful of hay and take a few determined steps towards the paddock.

"Oy! When did you get in?" Sam's voice peeks over my bundle and I look up, frowning in mock confusion.

"What do you mean?"

He looks over his shoulder, obviously perplexed, and I smile at him brightly when I pass him. "Must have just missed me while you were taking in the morning chatter."

Striding past, I catch the dumbfounded look on his face and snicker softly to myself.

Throughout the rest of the day, I shuffle my duties just enough to continuously position myself near all the visitors who come to the stables, in hopes of catching a whiff of gossip. The crisp, earthy, and pungent smells of a horse barn all mixing together, I wonder why the stables receive so many daily guests as opposed to many other parts of the castle. By the end of the day I've learned that the view of sweat-soaked, strong men hauling heavy straw bundles and nuzzling animals is a major attraction for more than a fair share of palace servants and townspeople the like.

The gossip-mill run by the visitors is on-going, current, and exciting, but I couldn't care less if the butcher passed out at the tavern last night, drinking heavily because his husband left him for the blacksmith... and I merely chuckle at the fact that one of the cooks found a rat in the kitchen and mixed it into the stew; I don't eat the food here.

As the sun seeks its rest for the night, I kiss the bridge of Curaidh's nose. "Sorry, my friend. I've only got one more day with you until the princess makes her decision and we've only been out for the one ride, so I don't know if she'll keep me around after this."

Big black eyes blink slowly at me and my eyes follow them, down the long, strong lines of his frame. "Do you miss it?" I ask him. "The feel of galloping, of racing towards the horizon? You must. You ran like hell a few days ago. What do you say one of these days we set off for a ride together? Take in a quick adventure across the kingdom, just to find a little bit of freedom?"

"I wouldn't do that, if I were you."

I jump at the voice, turning around to see Sam, chewing on an errant piece of straw. He shuffles one foot into the dirt, nodding his chin at the horse and I. "Stealing a horse that belongs to one of the princesses? You'd be on the headsman's block for sure."

I sigh, somewhat rolling my eyes. "I didn't intend to, Sam. Just feel bad for this gentle giant."

He snorts, a common mannerism for the Stable Master, and his eyes crinkle to show good will. "I never took you for much of a dreamer."

My lips tilt downward, frowning at the thought. "I'm not. Not really. I believe in action, doing rather than dreaming. But sometimes we don't know what to do unless we see it in our mind first."

"Well, lass, now you're a philosopher!" Sam howls laughter toward the sky, looking much like a pudgy wolf cub attempting a first call for its mother.

I laugh, more at him than at his joke, but I let him be none-the-wiser. "Have a good night, Sam."

He waves at me, walking off, still chortling to himself at his humor.

I settle Curaidh into his stall for the night and after saying goodbye, I leave the stable, wandering down to the street market. Still not safe to eat at the tavern, I purchase nightly meals from the many vendors who set up shop in the streets.

I'm absolutely famished tonight; skipping lunch to keep my nose hot on the information trail that didn't pan out to anything, I indulge in more food than I typically would, scarfing it down in an expedient fashion.

Halfway through attempting to swallow, my ears catch a familiar word on the wind, and I freeze: *curse.*

Two women walk arm in arm down the path not far from where I am seated, heads lowered and whispering conspiratorially. One grabs the other's arm and pulls her into the shadows, stopping to issue a warning to her friend.

"Ssh! Don't say that! You don't know what people will say about you if you start talking about magic like that!

"But I swear it's true. All those people missing... what do you think has happened to them? Where have they gone? And now this! This whole kingdom is under a spell, and the princesses are cursed, right at the very heart of it! I heard it from Mae who heard it from Agatha who heard it from Alanna and Alanna works with Caitlin in the castle and Caitlin was as white as a ghost when she talked about it!"

Gods, I love gossip.

"But that doesn't mean it's a curse. It's just odd, that's all. Coincidence."

The second girl sighs dramatically. "The king's gone mad about it. Locked them up all in one room to sleep together at night to see if he could stop it, but every morning is the same - their shoes are ruined, the princesses look gaunt and sickly, and they've turned the lot of them into cold-hearted empty-headed shells! I wouldn't be surprised if one of them died soon, the way I hear they're looking these days."

Her companion frowns in thought, brow furrowed to the point her eyes disappear. "That's terrible. I wonder if there's some sort of affliction in the castle." Eyes widening, she looks up at her friend. "I hope it isn't catching!" She steps back, putting a small amount of distance between them.

Unnoticed, the girl prattles on, fully invested in her story. "I hope it's Princess Mery that dies. She's a right bitch at times."

"Oh, but not Princess Meg. There never was a sweeter girl in the world."

"It's true." She sighs, leaning against the nearby wall. "I do wonder what will happen to the princesses. If I could only be a fly on the wall in their room at night. I'm sure the king would look kindly on anyone who could solve the mystery and restore the princesses to health and vitality!"

She mimics fitting a crown to her head and bursts out laughing, but I lose the rest of their conversation. Tossing my food aside, I slip away into the darkness, darting off towards the castle once more, and race into the stable.

I dash into Curaidh's stall, trying to be as still as possible. One eye cracks open and the horse huffs out a breath, nose tickling me a bit as I shimmy out of my dress and into my old, mended clothes. "That's more like it!" I whisper to the horse, who makes a noise like I would imagine a horse would make if it could roll its eyes.

Pinning my hair up, I kiss the end of his nose once more. "Wish me luck!" And with that, I swing myself upon the stable roof and race along towards the palace walls.

6

You can pack a lot of thoughts into a split second. At this very moment, I'm seriously debating my lack of wisdom. Impulsive isn't a word I would use to describe myself. Calculating? Yes. Observant? Absolutely. I plan things out as best I can in order to eliminate any and all variables. You've got to live this way if you want to be successful in my type of work. You've got to think ahead, prepare for every eventuality. Of course, you can't predict them all; so being adaptable and able to think - and move! - on your feet is vital too. But I always go in with a plan.

Right now, as I'm hanging by four fingers, fifty feet off the ground... I realize something. Something important. Something that might have been a good idea. I didn't make a plan.

I could have found another way into the castle, I'm sure. I could have disguised myself, lied about my identity, and conned my way in. Of course, I suppose the princess might have recognized me, so maybe that wasn't the best idea. Maybe I could have bribed a delivery man, stowed away in an ale barrel, and been smuggled into the castle kitchens. But then again, if a chef with a large butcher knife decided to sneak some drink before dinner, my days might have ended with no answers. Sighing loudly, I curse the situation I'm in. Maybe being reckless right now was the right way to go. It doesn't look like there's any other way into the castle without a heavy guard presence, and my well-honed climbing skills have gotten me this far.

Grimacing, I swing my left hand up, squinting my eyes shut as I grapple for purchase on a narrow ledge a few inches beyond my reach. Stretching to my fullest, I finally secure a grip but my muscles are screaming, straining with effort. To my right about 20 meters away there is a window. It's dark, so I'm trusting no one is in that room. I know my arms only have a few more minutes of strength left in them so I take a slow, steadying breath, and begin to cross the grueling distance.

When at last I reach the window ledge, I am soaked in sweat, fingers numb. I don't think I can go further, not only from the weakness I feel in my muscles but from all the dust on the stone wall ledges; my fingers feel slick and sticky all at once, no longer able to secure a tight hold.

Pushing myself up, I manage to get one elbow up into the window ledge, then the other. I puff my breath upwards, trying to remove a way-ward hair from my vision, when a flurry of movement in the corner of my eye catches my attention. Something is moving in the darkness. Something is coming towards me. My ears fill with the sound of scream-ing, and instinct causes my muscles to seize. I jolt backwards, my mind catching up one second too late.

You can pack a lot of thoughts into a split second. In other seconds, there's barely time for one.

This is how I die.

As if in slow motion, a flowing, willowy figure floats above me, moonlight reflecting off of soft white folds of fabric that seem to float in midair. I can hear the startled gasp of a woman's voice as my fin-gers slip from the windowsill. Pale cheeks and pink lips look down at me, framed in thick curly hair, and I close my eyes. She leans forward, reaching for me, and the action presses her breasts together - a perfect bosom, inches from my face.

Well, at least the view is good. I close my eyes, fixing the image in my mind, prepared to meet my fate.

The jolt that follows is a rude awakening, indeed. A searing pain suddenly rips through my shoulder, followed by my body slamming into something rough and hard. A flash of light pierces through my head, and suddenly I feel...nothing. Ah. I must be dead.

The throbbing in my head subsides, and I smile... then a voice from above whispers angrily at me, reassuring me that heaven still awaits.

"What are you doing?!"

Bleary eyed, I look up to see the princess - my princess - leaning out of the window, a bizarre expression on her face. She looks both bewildered and in pain - her eyes are bulging, lips pressed together in a firm line, and a thick vein pops down the middle of her forehead.

My eyes travel down her arms to see her hands clasped around my left wrist as I hang from her grip.

"I am going to drop you!" She hisses at me through clenched teeth and I look down, the far-off earth registering the reality of my situation and snapping me back to reality.

The pain in my shoulder triples and I bite down hard on my lower lip to keep a strangled cry from escaping. My head bursts anew with pain as the details of my current plight overwhelm me. This petite woman is the only thing keeping me between life and the demise of turning into a humiliating splatter. Taking a deep breath, I speak to her in the calmest voice I can manage.

"Plant your feet against the wall. On the count of three, you need to push against them and pull backwards as hard as you can."

She nods fervently, sweat beads trickling down the sides of her face.

"One... two... three!"

A horrific jolt of pain blinds me, but I throw my right arm up as I rocket forward, clasping the window ledge just in time to feel my left wrist slip from her grasp.

"Now, please... help me inside!" My voice is hoarse, and I can see the princess scramble upright and grab my shoulders. I yelp at the contact and she lets go quickly, a shocked sound tumbling from her lips. Shaking my head, I try and motion for her to come back to me. "No, please. I need your help. You have to pull me up."

Warily, she takes hold of me once more and with a grunt of exertion, pulls the top half of me in through the window, stumbling backwards. I fall the rest of the way in, crumpling into an unceremonious heap on the floor.

I take a few heaving breaths, but within seconds the princess is standing before me, a long silver knife half the length of a sword pointed directly at my heart, and a small candle clutched tightly in her other hand.

Brain still processing slowly due to recent events, I can feel my heart clench in fear... until I realize she's holding it all wrong. There's no balance in her stance, her hand is too far from the hilt, and she struggles to hold its weight in her hand; although that one, I'll give her. She did just pull me through a window four stories off the ground.

"What are you doing here? And why were you outside my window? And what were you trying to do? Why were you climbing the walls? *How* were you climbing the walls?"

The questions tumble out of her in one breath, so urgently I can barely make out each word. She waits the length of a deep breath, hands trembling under the weight of the weapon. "Well?"

I take a massive breath and wince in pain, opening my mouth to speak, but nothing comes out. How in the seven hells am I going to explain this one?

"I'll call the guards! They'll be here any minute!"

Realizing that she's not bluffing, I raise my good arm, palm open in surrender. "Yes, yes. Okay."

I slump against the wall, cradling my injured arm in my lap.

"I'm not going to hurt you. I have no intention of hurting you, or anyone else. I'm looking for answers. And I believe the castle is where I need to begin my search."

She frowns, brows furrowing so deeply they hide her amber eyes. "What sort of answers?"

"......Magical answers."

She rushes towards me, just stopping herself from pressing the sword to my skin, whispering loudly. "Ssshhhh! Don't say that!"

"Don't say what?"

"You know..." her eyes dart back and forth as if expecting people to materialize out of the thick stone walls. "Magic."

The perplexed expression I'm wearing must be significant because her whole face sours and she practically rolls her eyes at me. "Only a fool would ever mention that here, and in my presence too! My mother was killed by magic, and after her death, father outlawed all magic from the kingdom. Even the mention of it can land you in the fire. Why, I could have you killed!"

"You won't, though. Besides..." I shift a bit, trying to somehow get more comfortable, gasping through the pain. "I promised you that when the time came for me to tell you who I was... I'd be as honest as I could be. Luckily for you, that time has come sooner than I'd anticipated."

"It has?" Her eyes widen, sparkling, and she leans forward some in anticipation. The sword tip dips towards the ground and she stumbles, quickly finding her footing once more. She clears her throat, assuming a disinterested expression on her face.

"It has?" She repeats again, a forced flat tone to her voice.

I snort in laughter, but nod in defeat. "To put it simply, princess, I am not from Gormliath, and I don't know how I got here."

"What on earth do you mean?"

"I mean that on the day that we met, when I fell asleep I was in Oceanica and woke up in Gormliath; a fact I only discovered later."

The princess lowers the sword tip but keeps a firm grip on the handle. "But that's impossible!"

"So I thought myself. But here we are. I'm of sound mind and not prone to fantasy, yet clearly I am in Gormliath. The only conclusion I have left before me is magic."

She stares unblinkingly at me, but her face is much softer than before. "So then... you're an outsider?"

"It appears so. And I promise you, I have no intention of hurting anyone, especially not you. I was told that the palace was the seat of all of the old magic here in Gormliath, before it was outlawed. So here I am. I thought I was making my way to an empty room. My apologies for frightening you, your highness."

She frowns, still kneeling in front of me. Then she sighs dramatically, rocking back onto her heels. "Are you alright?"

"Not precisely, no. While I am and forever will be grateful to you for your rescue, I'm afraid my shoulder has been pulled from its joint and suffered a major injury." She opens her mouth, but I push forward, cutting her off. "I will be well again eventually. I know some things about healing. My..." I drift off, sure the less I tell her of my mother, the better. "...father taught me a little."

A gust of wind billows through the window and the princess shivers; it's only then that I realize how scandalously she is dressed. The ethereal white vision in my dreamlike state earlier is nothing more than her nightgown, resting gently upon naked flesh beneath.

I swallow, hard, and force my eyes to the ground. Searching desperately for anything to distract my attention, I push myself off the wall with grim effort and scoot closer to the large fireplace that fills the East wall. A few telltale embers still glow brightly near the back of the firebox, and there's a very subtle warmth radiating from the logs and ashes within.

"I should be able to get this started again easily." Lifting the small tin box nearby, I open it and snatch out the firesteel. The princess releases a startled cry and grabs hold of my hands, stopping the movement.

"No, please!"

Puzzled, I look at her, then back at the dead fire. "Aren't you cold? You're sitting here in the dark and you just shivered. I should-"

Her breathing is suddenly sharp, a tension coursing through her. She looks desperately between the fireplace and my hands and a question forms in my head. "Princess, did you put out the fire yourself?"

Wild eyed, she looks trapped, and I realize that I'm not the only one here with secrets. She looks absolutely terrified.

Holding her gaze steady, I cover her hands with my own. "Meg... what has you so frightened?"

7

〜

"I am NOT afraid!"

Her reaction is swift and angry and yes, absolutely afraid. She continues to whisper, voice just catching at high pitches with the force of her breath hissing between her lips. The princess snatches her hands away from me, wringing them in front of her before she puts them at her side, straightening her arms and clenching her fingers into fists. "I'm not afraid."

I purse my lips, pulling my eyes from hers, and notice the room we are in. The dim candlelight forms a small halo, reaching tendrils of light into the dark corners of the room. A small bed, with a mattress carelessly stuffed with straw, one small wooden chair, and a pewter chamber pot. This is no room of a princess.

"Where exactly are we?"

She looks up at me, moist eyes shining bright with the reflection of candlelight. "An old servant's room. It's been vacant for a while now."

"Okay..." Sensing I shouldn't push her, I try a different tactic. "Did you come here for the view?" She shakes her head, ebony ringlets dancing in front of her eyes with the quickness of the movement, but that's the sum of her response.

I chuckle at my own joke. "Probably best, seeing as how I ruined that experience this evening."

A hint of a smile peeks at the corners of her lips. Time to push a little further.

"I may not be a very wise individual, but based on what I'm seeing... are you, perhaps, hiding?"

She lifts her eyes to meet me, chewing at her bottom lip. "I was getting ready for bed... When my maids left me, I snuck away from the room. I came here."

"And... why are you here?" I ask the question hesitantly, trying not to pry but sure that this is significant somehow.

"I-" She cuts herself off and swallows, the fingers on one hand drumming against her thigh while the other remains tightly wound. "I didn't want to go to bed, just yet."

I must blink stupidly at her, openly perplexed by the seemingly immature nature of her statement, because she wrinkles up her nose and scowls at me. "Do not look at me like that! I am no longer a child, I am twenty-two!"

A quick laugh escapes my lips, and I look at her slyly. "There is not a soul in all of the Seven Sacred Kingdoms who doesn't know your age, your highness."

Her eyes fly open, shock and hurt crossing her face, and I realize the error in my words. "Forgive me. That was entirely the wrong thing to say. I am eternally sorry."

There is a long, awkward pause, and I sigh, leaning back against the wall, groaning as I shift incorrectly against my hurt shoulder. Her eyes lift to mine, and I grimace at her. "I can be an inconsiderate arse."

She slumps backwards, sitting with a soft 'thud' on the floor. "Do not concern yourself with it. I am... well, what else is there to say? I am the one whose very life is defined by the fall of the empire."

A soft smile decorates her beautiful face, but her voice has an edge of steel to it. When a concerned look floats over my face, she forces a laugh, but I cut her off. "There's nothing you did. You understand that, don't you? You didn't cause your mother's death any more than I caused mine's. You're not cursed or an ill omen or different from any other woman. You're just... You."

Meg's lips form a sad smile, and it almost feels as if she is mourning. "I most definitely am different."

"Granted, you are a princess and that's not a common thing in terms of the general population, I'll give you that."

She doesn't even smile. Instead, she looks at her toes, and wraps her hands around her bare feet. When she speaks, it is a whisper. "I am afraid of what happens when I sleep."

I tilt my head, taking in her words. "Do you mean you have nightmares?"

Once again she shakes her head in a flurry of curls and looks up to meet my eyes. "You were wrong, when you said I wasn't cursed. Things... happen. I fall asleep and when I wake up every night, my sisters and I, we-"

My eyes widen, and the gossip from this morning clicks into place. "You what?"

As if bewitched, she speaks urgently, frantically, and I can barely follow her words. "There's dancing, and a great feast, and the finest wine, and it's beautiful and I feel alive in the most terrifying ways! And then... And then I fall asleep again and none of it makes any sense and I have the most excruciating headaches and I-!" She cuts herself off, clutching the sides of her head as she rocks back and forth. "I don't know what's happening! It isn't a dream at all and yet I am not fully awake."

When she looks up, there are tears on her face. "It is all wrong! My sisters are gone. They are with me, but they are gone. They no longer live in their heads. They are empty shells, but when they do speak it is nothing but cruelty and mockery until at night we dance and drink and they are full of life and vitality once more. What is happening?" She begins to sob, her hands weaving into her hair.

I let a few minutes pass, both so she can gather herself and so my mind has time to digest this new information. Obviously, there is truth to the rumors that swirl around the princesses. Uma was right; there is magic here.

"Your highness... does this happen... every night?"

She nods slowly, her tears falling more quietly now.

"When did this begin?"

"A few months ago. It began the night of my sister Helene's thirty fifth birthday. Her husband, he was poisoned a week before! He'd been killed by a kitchen maid whom he'd been engaging with behind Helene's back. When he got tired of her, she slipped Meridian Night Powder into his wine.... Helene was in mourning, but... on the night of her birthday, she called the sisters together. It felt like we were little girls again, staying up late into the night, telling stories and laughing. We all fell asleep that night together. And we all had the same bizarre dream that night. And every night, ever since, that dream persists. My sisters don't remember it any longer. They do not see the night, and yet I see them there so clearly. I think I must be losing my mind; I cannot make sense of anything!"

She is shaking, voice barely holding onto coherent speech as her chin trembles and tears continue to fall from her eyes.

"Alright. Sshhh. Don't be afraid right now. You're not in your room, you're not sleeping. You're here. And right now you're safe."

She bites her lip fiercely, and I can see how hard she is working to control her emotions.

As her cries quiet, I slide my hand along her head, down the side of her face, and rest my fingertips just below her chin. Gently bringing her eyes up to meet mine, I give her a gentle smile.

"Thank you for trusting me. You had no reason to."

She sniffles, an embarrassed smile lighting up her face for a brief moment. "That's not entirely true. You saved me, you saved my horse, and you've taken excellent care of him. Anyone who can be trusted to care for an animal with such respect and affection can be trusted to care for a person." She pauses, holding my gaze steady. "And you believe in magic. That doesn't hurt."

I stare at her, caught off guard - which, I'll tell you, doesn't happen much. "You're an impressive woman, your highness. I bow to your greatness." Mockingly, I tip forward into an exaggerated bow from my seat on the floor, but a sudden lightning bolt of pain rips through my shoulder. Leaning back against the wall, I bite my lip to somehow quell the pain. Her eyes fly to me, worry clouding over her gaze.

"Can anything be done to fix your arm?"

"Yes, but I'm afraid I can't do it alone. I'll have to find my way out of the castle in the morning and find someone to help me."

An offended look most unbefitting of a princess crosses her face, and she practically snarls at me. "And who am I? Am I not a 'someone' who could help?"

"You, your highness, are first and foremost a princess, and there is no way I am asking a princess of all people to help!" Her mouth flies open, but I hold up a finger. "And secondly, look at you! You're a dainty little thing and I am highly suspect of any strength training you might have encountered during finishing school."

She rises to her feet, puffing herself up with indignancy, her need to exit quite clearly forgotten. "I just pulled you into this window! I think I have more than proven my strength to you. Or would you rather I have let you fall?"

"I only slipped because you startled me! And that sudden ability was adrenaline, princess, not any example of superhuman strength possessed in that tiny and delicate frame of yours."

"You are so rude!" She throws her hands up, placing one on her hip, the other pointing out of the window. "I can control Curaidh. I have the strength to ride him, and I have the strength to rein him in. I may be small, but I am not weak."

"Princess," I beg of her. "This is no small task. If you do not have the strength to do this fully, I may well never have use of my arm again."

Her face blanches at that, but she closes her eyes for a second, takes a determined breath, and opens them again.

"Let me help."

I let the words weigh in the air, wondering if she really can pull it back into the joint. She's correct in that she can manage her great beast of a horse, and I suppose she isn't the weakest creature I've come across. Her spirit has to stand for something.

"Alright, fine."

Her answering nod is sharp, lips drawn together in a tight line and eyebrows drawn together. "What do I do first?"

"Help me lie down flat on the ground, with room for you next to me." She moves to my side, cradling my neck in her arms, and eases me down to the cold floor. The breeze from the window brushes across my skin, a welcome sensation. I hadn't realized how much I'd been sweating and an involuntary shiver ripples across my skin.

"Now, come take my hand. Gently, like that. Can you press one of your feet here, against my ribs?"

Shyly, she slides her naked foot against the side of my chest, toes just touching the base of my breasts. "Is this right?"

Please, oh goddess, please, do not let that warm feeling in my cheeks be blushing. Sneaking a glance at the princess, her head is unnaturally low, and I have a feeling that our thoughts may mimic each other's.

"Yes, that's perfect. Now pull my arm just a little away from my body. Yes, just like that."

I take a massive deep breath, then stare into her eyes. "On the count of three, push against my ribs with your foot and pull as hard as you can towards you, but don't tug - just pull firmly and evenly."

Her head bobs up and down with unnatural speed.

"On the count of three. One... two... three."

A shock of pain radiates from my entire left side and I bite down on my arm to muffle the cry that bursts forth from my lips. A popping sound deep within my ear, a new pain in my ribs, and suddenly, the pain in my shoulder is much, much less.

"I did it!" The elated shout that greets me is jubilant, the princess's hands clasped together in front of her heart. "I can't believe I really did it!" She peers down over me, a triumphant smile on her face. "How are you feeling now?"

"Much better, surprisingly. Help me up, please?"

She does, easing me back into a sitting position while I cradle my arm across my body. Looking around the room, I nod to the pillow on the bed. "Can you pull out the stuffing, and toss me that fabric?"

Confused, she does what I say, and I bite down hard on the fabric, ripping it into two long straps.... or at least that's my intention. The fabric shreds, a poor excuse for material, and I can't make anything long and wide enough to fashion into a sling.

"What are you doing?" Thus far the princess has observed with interest, perched on the edge of the bed studying my failed efforts.

"I am trying to make a sort of bed for my arm. It needs to rest." I pause my futile work, and sigh in frustration, staring at the ceiling. I close my eyes for a brief second, but the sound of gauze tearing pulls at my attention, and I look up to see the princess ripping inches of fabric from the bottom of her nightclothes.

"Will this work?" She holds up a large swatch of cloth, awkwardly severed but sized in a way that I can utilize.

"Yes, thank you," I stutter, shocked by both the assistance and the display of her legs as they peek beneath the raised hemline.

Taking the gauze, I wrap it around my arm, and with her help we tie it into a rudimentary sling, enough to rest my arm. Once finished, she sits back, a soft smile on her face, and I look into her eyes.

"Thank you, by the way. I am afraid tonight puts me heavily in your debt."

A determined expression meets me, the curve of her jaw set in a stubborn line. "Then help me. Help me discover what is happening to me, to my sisters. Please. If you have any compassion or integrity, or a sense of duty to repay your life for another, please."

The moon, now high in the sky, adds a silvery light that stands in contrast to the dull orange glow provided by the candle. Luminescent rays fall on the princesses' pale skin, reminding me of the color found on the inside petals of a moon lily. A light blossom of color touches her cheeks, and her dark eyes glimmer beneath thick black lashes. Strikingly beautiful, she could easily be mistaken for the typical quiet, demure princess of so many stories; a damsel in distress, one who needs rescuing. And while she is asking for my help now, the fire that burns in her soul is one of wit and strength and bravery. What a beautiful creature.

Reaching out my hand to her, I place mine palm-up, a sign of good-faith. Placing her hand in mine, palm to palm, we entwine our fingers and I whisper above our clasped hands.

"I will."

Her eyes are focused on our hands, wrapped together, and I can feel my palms begin to sweat as the contact extends. Lips parted, she breathes quietly, and my eyes take in every dimple and curve of her soft, round face. My heart begins to race in my chest, and I grit my teeth. There will be absolutely no falling for a princess. None. That can only lead to disaster.

Knowing I must pull my hand away, my body betrays me and my thumb strokes over the back of her hand before slipping from her grasp. Our eyes meet and I clear my throat, but our awkward moment is broken by the sound of voices calling the princess's name.

With a gasp, her head snaps up towards the door and she quickly extinguishes the candle, huddling near me in a dark corner.

"They're looking for me." She states the obvious, speaking the way those who are terrified do; repeating the facts, finding something solid to acknowledge, feigning confidence and awareness of the situation. "They're looking for me, and I'm here. With you." Suddenly her eyes fly open and she panics. "You're here! And I'm with you! If they find you, they'll kill you!"

Turning to me, she grabs the sides of my legs, a pleading look on her face. "You said you would help me, yes? You said you would help me discover what was happening..."

She closes her eyes, takes a deep, steadying breath, and when she looks at me again, her eyes are brimming with determination and defiance.

"Meet me at dawn, at the base of the great ashe tree." And with that, she rushes out the door.

8

Stunned, I sit there, trying to digest what happened. Did she run away, willingly returning to the thing that terrifies her so, in order to protect me? The thought is a sobering one, and I realize just how much she is placing her trust in my ability to solve whatever riddle plagues her.

How, though? With so little detail and information, I am lost. I can only hope that there is more to learn tomorrow. First, I need to figure out how to get out of here.

Having never been in the castle before, this proves a challenge. The halls outside are quiet; I can only guess the princess has found her way to those looking for her, and I shudder a bit as I recount the look in her eyes, thinking of what she must be going through in this moment. Getting ready for bed alongside her sisters, tucking herself in, and then... who knows?

I wait a quarter of an hour longer, ensuring the search party has entirely moved on. Finally content in the quiet outside the door, I creep towards it and open it slightly, staring into the darkness. Letting my eyes adjust, I notice a hint of light below me, and the rough outline of stairs comes into view, curving counterclockwise as they descend. Pulling my boots off, I tie the laces together and sling them over my good shoulder, praying for my footsteps to be muffled. I creep through the door and slowly begin to descend.

The light grows, and I hold my breath, calculating. Knowing it could be a torch held by a person or an unattended wall sconce, I study the pattern of the light on the walls; it dances gently, but there are no sudden movements, no changes in the direction of the shadow.

Thinking I'm safe, I take six more steps, quicker now, down the stairs.

Rounding another curve, I slam into the plump, soft rear of a well-endowed-everywhere woman. She yelps in surprise, and a rough baritone voice answers her.

"Don't shout, Hilde! I'd rather not get a lashing for getting caught!"

Standing beneath a torch on the staircase's outside curve are two lovers, failing miserably at concealing the true nature of their secretive evening tryst. Apparently-Hilde shoves her hands down the front of her skirt, trying to remove the man from momentary pleasures, still staring at me slack jawed and with eyes the size of silver coins.

Seizing the opportunity, I casually saunter by, roughly slapping the man on his shoulder. "Nice night for it, eh, man?" I drop my voice to its lowest pitch, hoping between their confusion and the speed of my exit that they assume I'm a man.

I stride down a few more steps lightly, but once I'm sure I'm out of view, I take the stairs two at a time, praying the seclusion sought by the lovers grants me the privacy I need to find my way out.

At the base of the stairs there is a thick wooden door, and I open it a crack, scanning the corridor beyond it.

The hallway is narrow, multiple doors lining each wall. Too few torches placed sparingly give an eerie glow, with no end in sight in either direction.

My eyes roll so deeply I can practically see my brain. Why must I always stumble upon an absence of clues when I need an exit?

Drawing a deep breath, I point my ears to each side of the hallway. Slightly muffled sounds to the right.... Absolute silence to the left.

Deciding that the sounds indicative of people mean a more centralized part of the castle, I creep through the doorway and tuck myself close to the wall, moving to the right.

Forty or so feet along, I can see a large oak door with iron hinges set into the wall to my left. Such an imposing, well-crafted door stands out in comparison to the small, simple doors that have dotted the hall thus far.

I creep over to it and press my ear to the wood.

Muffled voices come from within, and while I cannot make out a word of what they are saying, the voices are agitated and varying in volume. Mmm.. must be a few men with very hot tempers.

A shuffling sound just on the other side of the door causes me to step back suddenly, and not a moment too soon. The door comes flying open, missing my nose by a quarter of an inch.

Light spills into the hallway and a serving maid pushes past me carrying a tray filled with empty mugs of ale and a few half-eaten rolls of bread. The voices clamor, chaos ringing through the air before the door slams shut.

"Oh!" The serving girl looks at me with surprise, then her eyes settle on my shoulder and a sympathetic look slides over her features. "Poor thing... Arm must be hurting something fierce. Off to the kitchen for a quick nab before bed, are ya?"

I smile my most beguiling smile, laughing softly.

"You caught me. Hilde told me there was still some hot food."

Her responsive look is bright and she giggles, a sweet little laugh that reminds me of a cardinal in winter.

"Maybe there was before she ran off to find Martin, but I'm sure it's all been picked through by now! Ah well, I'm sure we can find you something simple to eat all the same."

She moves down the hallway, and assuming I'm supposed to follow, I trail after her, taking on the air of someone who is meant to be there. She chatters incessantly on all sorts of menial topics, and I reply with all the appropriate noncommittal grunts and vague agreements. Eventually the end of the hall comes into view, and another large set of stairs. Lifting her tray high so as to see her steps, she continues at her quick pace down the steep descent until finally we reach a small landing at the base of the steps. The only thing before us is a large door, heat emanating from it like a boiler. Approaching it, she turns around and pushes the door open with her bottom, stepping back so I can enter.

The kitchen fires are burning mightily, one on either side of the wide room, fireplaces large enough for me to stand in roaring mightily as the flames lick the stone walls.

"Och, are ye setting the coals for morning already?" The girl with me seems as surprised as I am to see the fires in such a state this late in the day, and a man I assume to be a cook rubs sweat from his brow.

"King's asked for a hunt in the morning. 'E wants to be up at sunrise." The scorn in his voice is positively potent.

"Of course he did." My companion sighs, setting down her tray and rubbing her hands on her apron. "He's bristling with so much anger these days it's no wonder he's wanting to kill something!"

She crosses to a large barrel and buries her arm elbow deep within, emerging with a small piece of fruit. She plucks a small tart off a nearby table and hands the two to me.

"There. Now off you go. Back to bed before Crowley spots ya!"

I grin my thanks. "I'm grateful! I'll just nip out the back for a drink of water then I'll be back in bed before anyone's the wiser."

Moving towards the door in the corner of the kitchen, I nod once to the chef, and with a wink to my savior, I step out into the cool night's air.

A quick second to understand my surroundings shows a path moving in two directions. One deep breath in the air and I catch the familiar whiff of horse manure.

Slipping off into the darkness towards the stables, I walk along a stone wall, trying to memorize all of the details around me. How can I find my way back to the kitchens for easy access to the castle once more?

Coming around a bend I find myself nearing a gate, guarded by two men. I slink back into the darkness. The guards are heavily armored, I suppose at the order of a paranoid king. I could slip past them somehow; backtrack towards the castle and find a way to scale the wall. But with my arm, and knowing there is safety in recognition, I decide my best bet is to make myself known.

Lurching out of the shadows, I stumble towards the guards, an incoherent tune dancing from my lips. Waving my fruit in the air like a well-drunk mug of ale, I vary my volume as wildly as my steps.

Pretending to see the guards for the first time, I stop suddenly, smiling broadly.

"Good morning, gentlemen!" Pausing to 'think' with dramatic effect, I consider my words. "Night. It is night, isn't it? Ha!"

One of them eyes me warily while the other tries to hide a smile. "Who are you, then? And what are you doing here?"

"Who am I? Why... I'm me!" I stand tall, tossing my head back. "I was in sore need of dinner, my friends... sore need." Shaking my head somberly, I lower my gaze but just manage to catch the second guard tuck his hand over his lips as his shoulders begin to quake. "Curaidh was a right bastard today, near ripped my arm right off!" I sway dramatically for emphasis, leaning towards the two guards. "I took a few drinks to ward off the pain but wouldn't you guess, a few turned to a few too many and now I can't figure out how to find my way back to the stables."

For extra effect, I slump onto the ground, sitting limply.

"Dammit, this must be the lass that works in the stables," the giggly one says.

Lifting my eyes, I stare up at them, channeling my inner kitten-face. "Do... you know how to get there?"

Two slow blinks. Then I wait. Works every time.

Angry Guard sighs and grabs my good arm, lurching me to my feet. Shoving me through the gate, he points along the dirt road before me. "Stay straight on the road and you'll stumble there before morning."

"Aye, then! I am forever grateful!" I can't help myself, so when the path curves to the right I keep walking straight, stumbling into the grass.

"Och, for fuck's sake!" shouts the guard. "I didn't mean straight... literally!"

"Ooooooooh!" Finding my way onto the path again, I continue on my way until I know I'm out of earshot and sight.

At last, the stables come into view, and I breathe a sigh of relief.

9

Chewing on the thick stem of a cana-palm isn't my favorite, but the pain that radiates all over my body makes it thoroughly worth it. The base of the ashe tree makes for a comfortable spot and I sit, mashing the rubbery plant with my teeth until I can slurp the bitter juices from within. Burgeoning sunlight filters over the land, and I watch as it creeps at an achingly slow pace towards the tips of my boots. Just as I point my toes towards the orange glow, a shadow falls upon them.

Startled, I scramble to my feet, hastily sucking in the pulp on my lips and rubbing a sleeve across my face. The princess stands before me, an amused look hiding the exhaustion plain on her face.

"Good morning, your highness," I murmur, bowing my head to her.

"Good morning."

I look up, and her eyes follow me, curious. They settle on my lips, and she stares for a moment too long. A nervous laugh escapes my lips and I turn my head to the side. Opening my mouth to ask how her night was and if she is okay, she cuts me off.

"What were you eating?" She now looks at the remnants of the stem clutched firmly in my palm.

I hastily shove the plant behind me, winking at her. "Just a little pain relief to get me through the day, Princess." Giving her a bright smile, I try to distract her from my own woes. "Don't worry about it, though. I'll be feeling perfect in just a few minutes. Tell me about your night."

She holds out a large empty basket, ignoring my inquiry. When I give her a puzzled look, she shakes the basket in her hand, pushing it towards me. Taking it from her, she exhales a gust of breath, and gives a quick, firm nod before turning and striding away. "We're going for a walk." She looks at me, pleading. "Come with me."

I follow her silently, unsure of the proper protocols. Do I stand beside her? Just behind? Do I lag much further behind? My steps are disjointed and I'm sure I look foolish trying to figure out the distance between us.

Forty paces down the road, she turns and looks at me with an annoyed look on her face. "What precisely are you doing?"

"Uuhhh..." *Such wit, such grace!* Clearing my throat, I try again. "Exactly how far behind you am I supposed to be walking?"

"Oh. Come a little closer." I take a few steps. "More..." she beckons me even closer. "It's a bit more..." I inch forward a tad and she grabs my hand and pulls me to her side so I am standing level with her. "You know, you can be very clever, and you're obviously strong for a girl, but in addition to being whom I assume to be a scoundrel, you're also a bit daft!"

Balancing on her tiptoes, she bops the top of my head, then continues on down the road, waiting for no one.

Without time to digest whatever that was, I rush forward again, this time falling in step beside her. Even with her determined pace, she seems to glide along the road, appearing every bit a princess regardless of her attire. Thus far I've seen her adorned in frills and lace, pearls hung round her neck, in a sturdy riding gown, and in the thin silk of her nightgown last night that clung so perfectly to her curves... *Nope. Stop that. Don't think about that; about how my hands could fit perfectly against the swell of her hips, how her breasts are low but full, tiny budded nipples pointing slightly downward...*

"Are you ill? You look awfully red." She's glancing up at me, and I suck in a breath realizing the course my thoughts have travelled.

"I'm fine. Just something that happens with that particular remedy," I lie quickly.

"Oh. I understand." She eyes my shoulder in its sling and tugs her lower lip into her mouth with a frown. "I'm glad to see you made it out of the castle alright. I was awfully worried about you."

I snort out a laugh, stepping just in front of her to steer her out of the way of a muddy puddle in the street before us. "You? Worried about me?"

Now it's my turn to see the hint of a blush creep up along her cheeks. "I was - well, it was... later. This morning. When I woke up I was thinking of our meeting and I was - "she pauses, searching for the right word. "Concerned, that's all."

"I see. Well, I thank your highness for your concern. I was concerned about you, as well."

She makes a thoughtful noise, but there is nothing else from her. I offer her my arm, and she takes it with slight hesitation. We walk in silence through the castle-town until we reach the large gate. As we near the guards, I notice her posture stiffen and I can feel a palpable shift in her energy, transforming her into someone regal, almost untouchable. Remembering just who this woman is, the beloved daughter of the king... the little buzzing in my stomach ceases almost immediately.

I try to adjust my poise, wanting to look like I belong by her side and to avoid notice of or questioning by the guards. They don't even blink at the two of us as we make our exit.

Not long after we pass through the gates, the princess veers off the road and down a small path worn into the tall grasses that dress the hillside outside the castle town. "Lovely day for picking berries, don't you think?" She looks to the sky, squinting as the sun begins a slow climb into the sky, then sends me a significant look.

"Yes, indeed it is. Curaidh will surely adore them as a treat later this afternoon."

She beams at me, happy that I've caught on. "Through that wood over there is a beautiful glen filled with the sweetest blackberries I've ever tasted. They're a favorite of his, too."

Letting go of my arm, she begins to wander a bit, moving between patches of wildflowers like a butterfly searching for an afternoon treat. As we tread across the grasses, I am grateful that I am still in my pants.

I study the princess's movements as she struggles to navigate her footing and tugs at her the folds of her skirt when brambles from nearby bushes fasten to the length of her dress. Once I am sure the castle is far enough away that the specifics of our movements are hidden, I call to her.

"Princess?" I hear her sigh before she turns, trying to hide her frustrations. "I believe I have a solution for the difficulties your attire might be giving you."

When she doesn't respond, I move closer to her and kneel at her feet. "May I?"

Silently, she nods her head, and I get to work. She's wearing a simple dress today, far more 'berry picking' than 'royal ball' - but it is still the dress of royalty. Multiple layers of fabric ripple down her figure, and it takes a second for me to find the shape of her legs beneath them. My fingers brush against her bare skin at one point and I hear a sharp intake of breath from above me. "Sorry," I mutter quietly.

Within a few minutes, I have her many skirts fashioned into a sort of bloomer-like assemblage, tied round her thighs and ankles with some of the many lengthy blades of grass. There are quite a few embarrassing moments as I shape them together, but I keep my head down and act as if I've played tailor many times before.

"Are you sure you know what you're doing?" she asks me. The tone of her voice is strained, and every muscle in her body is strung tightly.

"Getting tired, your highness? I would think a lady of your station is used to enduring fittings of greater length and frustration." I cannot help the teasing quality of my voice, and I look up at her, quirking one eyebrow at her to match my smirk.

"You're so rude!" She huffs her breath out and crosses her arms across her chest as I tie the final laces.

"That may be, Princess, but who else could have made you these?" Sliding back into a crouch, I gesture towards her new attire. "Here we are."

She hesitantly looks down and rolls her lips together, pursing them tightly as she gingerly lifts one foot a few inches into the air, staring at her ankles.

"Princess, you're not testing out a brace for a broken leg, it's just... Well, it's as close to trousers as I can get."

Embarrassed, she lets out a breathless chuckle, before taking a few slow steps around.

Giggling to myself, I rise and turn away to give her privacy of discovering her new attire, dusting my hands off on my stomach. Suddenly there's a rushing sound, followed by a loud whoomp!... and I realize she's hugging me.

"These are amazing! Thank you so much!" Her arms wrapped around my middle, she looks up at me, eyes shining.

Mesmerized, I can't help but say the thing so present in my starstruck eyes. "You're so... little." *Ah yes. My inner poet reveals herself once again.*

She cocks her head at me, puzzled, then her eyes travel downwards until she's staring straight ahead, taking in a close-up of my collarbone. She swallows loudly, and after an agonizing beat, shivers out of my arms. "We're almost to the woods."

Turning, she rushes off at a lively pace. Any unease she was feeling after our little encounter and teasing melts quickly away as she delights in the newfound freedom of her movement. I can hear little flirts of laughter lilting through the air in her wake as I follow after, and I cannot help but smile. What an exhilarating woman. The rapidity of her emotions is dizzying, and yet admirable. Never long to let something keep her down, she sees so much light in a world that I assume holds many dark secrets.

At the edge of the forest, the grasses thin and give way to a few yards of dry soil before trees begin to tower above us. It appears never ending; the sort of forest one can easily enter and never leave, but the princess seems certain of herself, forging ahead with deliberate, even steps.

All at once, a seed of insecurity curls inside my stomach. What if this is all a ruse? What if she knew that tricking me would be the only way to secure me long enough for an arrest? I know she's clever, but perhaps I have underestimated the extent of her mind.

Cursing myself and the situation, I feel anxious. I've let myself become taken in by her wit and bravery, but goodness. As someone who has performed more than my share of trickery... what if she is tricking me?

She spins around and looks at me impatiently. "Come on, then."

Masking my worries with a smile, I walk towards her. "Where exactly are we going?"

"That way." She speaks as if everyone knows it is 'that way', shrugging her shoulders a bit in emphasis. "We've got to move East through the forest. It's the shortest way to the glen. We should be able to talk there."

Moving forward once again, she sets off and I follow after, eyes and ears alert for the slightest indication that we are not alone.

"May I ask you a question?" She chirps up, a few minutes later.

"I suppose," I respond warily, knowing I need to stay alert.

"You told me that you went to sleep in Oceanica and woke up here in Gormliath. Is that where you're from?"

"No," I answer hesitantly. "I was born in Nerogaia. My father raised herds of sheep in the Nerogaian mountains. I am the daughter of a shepherd." Conveniently leaving the specifics of my mother's work out, I make an addition though I'm not entirely sure as to why. "I come from far more humble beginnings than you do, your highness."

She makes a face that in our few interactions I've already come to realize is the expression she wears while considering something deeply. "What happened, then? Why were you all the way in Oceanica? Did you have a family there?"

When one must lie, always lie as closely to the truth as possible; or in some cases, tell the truth - but omit a few key details. "My father died when I was very young. My mother disappeared just when I was eight. I did my best for a few years, but there was no reason to stay, and no way to afford it either."

"Oh, how awful. What a terrible life you have led thus far." She looks genuinely remorseful, a full bouquet of pity written all over her face.

"It wasn't terrible."

"But you have nothing! And you sleep in..." She searches her memory furiously, brows furrowed deeply. "You sleep in trees! And you steal for your food!"

My reply is more bitter than I had anticipated, and even I am shocked at how vitriolic I sound, but this is a wound long festering and I find myself growing agitated and forget for a split second the situation I am in.

"I know that from your silk dresses, well-stoked fires, and fluffy down mattresses your view of the world must be one of comfort, but I have no regret over the life I have lived. We are not the masters of our fate, but we can influence it if we know how. I lost my family, yes. But I made the choice to live on the road, and I made the choice to find my own way in the world, and yes, even I made the choice to be here with you today, princess. So please, take the pity you feel for me and throw it aside, because I don't need it or want it. The life you imagine I could have is nothing but a nice dream, and will never be more than that."

There is a drawn-out stony silence as the two of us glare at each other. Her skin has flushed red, and her lips are drawn to a flat, thin line. When she finally speaks, it is careful and measured though I can hear emotion brimming through her words.

"It would do you well not to talk of soft beds and pleasant dreams to me."

A hint of moisture plays at the corner of her eyes, and I realize that I've touched a sensitive nerve. The entirety of the purpose of this venture through the woods was to address this so-called issue that I promised I would help with. What a stark contrast twelve hours can have on a person.

"You are correct, Your Highness. I will guard my words more carefully." I incline my head to her, my tone and posture dripping with formality.

"Indeed you shall!" The words fly from her lips as she tries to get them out as quickly as she can. Stepping past me, her chin is held abnormally high as she tries to assume a haughty expression, but I don't miss the telltale quiver of her chin.

10

Five minutes later we are still on our journey, a stony silence heavy in the air between us. Everywhere I look I see trees and nothing more. My nerves are thrumming within me, the fever pitch tightening every muscle. *Relax the shoulders, roll out the neck... don't be too tense. You can't fight if you're too tense.*

I am actively perplexed by this situation. I am certain that if the princess was truly luring me into a trap, she would be doting on me, laying on affections to keep me engaged. Storming ahead with a frosty expression on her face is not quite the way I'd keep someone following me, especially if I need their help... and it's also not the way I'd guarantee someone stay near me if I needed to ensure their capture. To make this even more bizarre, and even somewhat comical, I can hear her talking quietly to herself at times. The inflection of her words rises and falls as if she is scolding herself or arguing a point against her better demons, and she follows these monologues with a rough shake of her head or a sigh.

On we trudge, my mental calculations ticking off in rapid succession as I piece together the time we've been in the forest, when we met this morning, and how long it took us to get to the forest edge. If there is a plan in place, I wonder how much our pause to adjust her skirts has slowed us down, and if her storming ahead now is an attempt to make up for it. Lifting my eyes to observe the way she is walking once again, I notice now that her behavior has slowly changed. Now less dramatically frustrated, her movements are now something far more alarming; walking slowly, the princess is looking around.

Based on the movement of her head, I can tell her eyes are skimming the trees high and low, meticulously observing her surroundings. She scans the forest with a keen gaze, but her posture suggests she's purposefully wanting to appear nonchalant. The tense set of her shoulders magnifies the miniscule flinching she makes as she darts her eyes back and forth. But the thing that terrifies me the most about all of this? It is absolutely silent.

Not a single sound floats through the air so deeply in this forest. No animals scurrying about, no softly babbling brooks, no trees swaying in a gentle breeze.

This is absolutely, undoubtedly a trap.

Shit.

Take a deep breath, think clearly, and above all, don't let her see that you have her figured out.

Setting aside the desire to chastise myself for being so taken in by a pair of perky breasts and a charming smile that I missed the signs of being conned, I evaluate my choices at this point. Like any good thief, I know that offense is the best defense, and I'm not about to take any more chances.

Twenty paces ahead is a tree broader than the rest, only two paces from its closest neighbor; the start of good cover. Planning my escape, the second I reach it I slip behind its wide trunk, hiding from view. Careful to keep quiet, I sneak from tree to tree, slowly distancing myself from the princess, each step taking me farther and farther away.

I move with stealth, grateful for the dull earth tones of my pants and vest. Grabbing some dirt from the forest floor, I rub it quickly into my sleeves and sling, hoping to mask even more of the white fabric. Backing slowly away, maintaining my cover, my eyes dart in every direction. *Don't lose sight of her just yet, don't lose track of your path, don't lose concentration.*

Damn. I wish I'd slept more than a few hours or eaten something this morning.

Keeping one eye trained on her figure as I slip between the trees, I know that losing her is only half my battle; escaping the forest without capture is a whole different endeavor.

That's when I hear it. A single snapping sound, echoing through the forest as it bounces from tree to tree. The princess's head whips up, a startled gasp audible even to me.

She looks around, body moving frantically as she realizes I am no longer with her.

"Wh-where'd you go?" There is panic in her voice, and I grit my teeth at the sound of it. "Please! Where are you? I still need your help! This isn't a joke! Please, come back to me!" Of course the girl is lying. If she is truly scared, she wouldn't be shouting for me. She'd know that silence is vital, and concentration is key... wouldn't she?

Then - another snapping sound behind me and I whip my head around in the direction of the noise. A man drops out of the treetops, landing at my feet with a very soft thud.

If you've ever been startled - truly, genuinely shaken - you'll know that you can collect a thousand minute details in less time that it takes to blink an eye or inhale a breath. The man crouched in the dirt at my feet is long and lean, a sinewy creature covered head to toe in dark green wrappings. His face is smudged with dirt, and he smells atrocious, as if he's covered himself in some sort of animal feces. He wears no shoes, toes spread open against the grass to help him maintain his balance. Almost as quickly as his landing, he springs into the air, unsheathes a knife, and brings the butt of the handle down hard onto my temple.

An explosion of pain ripples across my skull as I crumple to the ground, and I hear a splitting scream tear through the air. Forcing my eyes to open, I see a flash of color, and I can just make out the blurred form of the princess, caught in the rough arms of two more attackers. Another crash of pain flies across my forehead, and everything goes black.

*****

What... the FUCK... is that godforsaken sound?

Breathing deeply, pain in magnitudes I have never known sears through my skull and shoulder. A groan slips past my lips and I pause, trying to collect the very jumbled thoughts that are materializing in my brain. Then I hear the sound again, reverberating through my head like the church bells that ring at the cathedrals in towns all across the Great Empire. This hurts!

My right eye won't open, so I gingerly twist my body around, rolling onto my back. Cracking open the left eye, a very, very large crow comes into focus, beady little eyes flicking back and forth as it observes me, cocking its head side to side. "CAW!"

"Bugger off!" I limply wave an arm at it and it simply hops backwards, out of reach of my fingers yet still fascinated by my presence.

"Bugger... off..." My voice trails off, a distinctive lack of strength in my body making it difficult even to speak. I blink slowly and I see, directly above my head, the distant tops of trees. A forest. I'm in a forest?

Lifting my good hand, three fingers softly explore my face, finding a bloody upper lip and a fat, blackened eye, at least to the touch. Gingerly testing out the rest of my limbs, I raise my legs a few inches off the dirt. Satisfied that I'm at least still mobile, I turn my head to the other side, away from the crow. Something small and green catches my attention, fluttering gently in the dirt. Inching along towards it on my side, I drag myself through the mud towards the object. My speed quickens as I get closer, dread coiling bitterly in my stomach. A small strip of green fabric lies in the dirt.

The princess!

I fly upright, sitting straight- then clutch at my head as the pain overwhelms me. Lurching forward, I retch onto the forest floor, vision popping with bright colors.

Once the bile ceases its exit, I stagger to my feet, clutching at my abdomen. My visitor apparently enjoyed a few kicks to my ribs before making his exit, and I add this to the list I'm keeping in my head of injuries to repay someday.

Crossing the forest, relying on trees for support, I come to a spot in the dirt where a struggle clearly took place. Long grooves in the earth look like someone was pushed or slid, footprints mashed over one another indicate a scuffle, and there's even one spot where a few drops of blood litter the ground. *Please, please - do not let that be hers.*

I do my best through blurred vision and pounding headache to assess the scene, but it's then that I notice a long, wide channel in the dirt; someone was dragged through here and based on the number of footprints on either side leading out of the forest, I am certain it was the princess.

I race after the path, ignoring the pain, desperate to find any sign at all of where they might have taken her. My thoughts are in freefall as my senses are overwhelmed with my last moments; flashes of her face looking absolutely terrified, the scream that vibrated through my bones, and how I left her, so certain she was betraying me.

My legs are moving at top speed, carrying me along through the forest in search of her. Finally, the path I follow changes and the trees clear; the glen, with blackberry bushes galore, appears before me. A beautiful sight, and yet all I feel is guilt. My hope is fading; but here, the telltale ruts of carriage wheels are buried deep into the dirt along the edge of the forest.

Keeping as close to the tree line as possible, I continue after the path. A carriage with wheels this wide is a fast one. They're clearly far beyond me, moving at a speed I'll never be able to match. My only hope is if they stop somewhere, so I slow my pace, as alert as I can be, knowing I might be watched. I need to save her. I must. But I can only help her if I'm alive.

After what feels like hours the adrenaline is wearing off and I am aching in every corner of my body, but a small stone cottage sits just ahead, a peculiar white smoke curling from its crooked chimney.

On a typical day, I'd consider this a quaint, charming setting. The house is nestled amongst honeysuckle bushes, sunlight streaming down upon it. Purple flowers crawl on vines up the stone walls, and the dark wooden door rests off balance on rusting hinges.

Today is not a typical day. A sinister miasma permeates the air and I immediately suck in my breath, tucking into the cover of nearby trees. The oppressive atmosphere feels heavy on my limbs, and I find myself feeling drowsy.

Spotting the smoke that rises, ethereal tendrils reaching for the sky, I pull my shirt up over my mouth and nose, breathing only through its filter. My head clearing somewhat, I narrow my eyes and focus.

There are people in the cottage. Shadows cross back and forth, blocking out the fire's light as it creeps under the door. Low voices in deep tones mumble slightly to one another, but there's no sounds of distress, and no voice with the clear high tones like those of the princess.

She's either dead, silenced, or no longer here.

Reaching under my shirt, I slide out my dagger and grip it firmly in my hand. In the realm of small blessings, I'm grateful that the attackers had no interest in robbery; both my coin purse and my dagger are in place.

Shifting a few paces to my left, then to my right, I can see no one outside the small building, nor anyone on the roof. A lengthy approach might catch unwanted attention, and there's no way I can peek inside the building. Silently cursing the very fact that I woke up today, I tighten my hold on my knife, hold it at the ready, and break off into a sprint towards the cottage door.

I I

With all of the momentum I have gathered, my foot makes solid contact with the door, breaking the rusted hinges as it crashes into the room. A cry of surprise hits my ears as three men stumble to their feet, slowly and lacking in coordination. A pungent odor assaults my nose and I feel instantly light-headed. Swearing loudly, I pull my shirt up over my nose once more, observing the space. My attacker from the forest stands before me, flanked by two burly men. Three pairs of eyes stare at me, glassy and blinking in slow succession.

"She's alive!" The closest man seems dumbfounded to see me, his mouth filled with food hanging open.

"I didn't kill her." The man in green stares at me, calculating eyes tracing me from my feet to the top of my head, before a smirk slides into place on his face. Lifting a finger, he points in the general direction of my blackened eye. "That's a good look for you, though, eh?" Reaching for me, I swat his hand out of the way and he loses his balance, stumbling.

"Where is she?" Refusing to banter, I grit my teeth and demand an answer. "Where is the princess?"

"We don't know." He shrugs, seemingly unbothered. "Got paid to snatch her and bring her here. That's what we did, then. Some bloke came and grabbed her and took off with her, and a good thing too. She knocked one of my teeth out." He lifts the corner of his mouth with a grimy finger, revealing the swollen bloody socket halfway along his upper jaw.

A tiny surge of relief courses through me, but I know it's for little good reason. Attempting to remain subtle, I peer around the room. Larger than I initially realized, the space is mostly barren, but a large coin purse, a sack of food, and a hefty jug of mead sit on the table. Must have been a substantial payday for capturing the princess.

Turning my gaze firmly back to the man, my voice comes out low and coarse. "Who did you hand her off to? Give me a name!"

"Don't know his name. Wish I did, though. When I took this job, he offered me riches beyond compare. Said it'd set me and my crew up for life! Well, look at this." He hikes a thumb over his shoulder to point at the wealth of goods on the table, a sour expression on his face.

"That lousy sod should have paid me better. But I never let anyone short me." He flips something up into the air and catches it cleanly. Turning it in his hand, he proudly shows off his steal. "This outta fetch me a fair price in the Smuggler's Den." A silver button, intricately patterned with the outline of a crow, a tiny emerald set into the button as the eye.

A wave of nausea hits me and again, a vacant feeling flashes through my brain. Glancing at the fire, I notice that tucked against the back of the fire, almost buried, the telltale purple flowers of the *somnus aeternum* are burning.

Somebody wanted these men to die. I'm sure they haven't noticed the toxin slowly filling the air; they are in no hurry. And I imagine they wouldn't take kindly to learning they're on someone's kill list. Not wanting to stick around for either of those realizations to come true in my presence, I decide it's time for me to leave,

"Well, then, gentlemen... if you cannot provide me with any other assistance, I'll be going now. Thanks again for the new facial arrangement."

I bow low with sardonic wit, and back up towards the door.

The man in green slowly slides a knife out from a sheath on his hip.

"It's really a pity. I could have used a woman of your talents on my team-" the man's expression morphs into a sneer "-but I'm afraid I have to kill you now." The words are barely out of his mouth before he charges at me.

The flower's effects have been taking their toll; his movements are nothing like the limber, stealthy attacks in the woods. He's moving clumsily, and takes a half second more than he should to reach me. Trying to dodge towards one side, I can see what he's doing. As he moves alongside my injured shoulder, he thrusts his arm out at me.

This is gonna hurt.

I can feel his blade slice across the side of my arm, but I hold steady, sacrificing the injury to complete my move. Shifting my stance to allow his follow through, I take the opportunity found in his now unprotected position. Honing in on the narrow indent at the base of his throat, I turn my wrist and lunge forward, sinking my dagger cleanly into the thin flesh just below his adam's apple. Turning away from him, my blade exits at an angle, and the man crumples to the ground at my feet, his knife clattering to the ground.

A rushing sound to my right alerts me to an incoming attack, and I spin, bending backwards as a fist glances against the outside of my cheek. As the assailant flies past me, I rip my arm through the air, two quick slashes across the side of his neck. I jump out of the way as he too falls, and face my final adversary.

It's been a long time since I've killed anyone. *I really fucking hate this.*

My last opponent is a giant. There's no other word for him. He stares at me with a demented smile on his face, and I reassess my stance. With another deep breath, I begin to lose focus. Shaking my head for a split second, I grab a flagon of mead on the nearby table and quickly douse the fire, sticky purple leaves sizzling into ash.

The giant blinks stupidly and rolls up his sleeves, an impressive scowl on his face. Wondering how I'll ever kill this man with only one arm, I duck my head and look at the floor behind him. The glimmer of a plan blooms in the back of my head. With no other time to think, I close my eyes and set my shoulders for a split second, wondering if this will be my last.

Pounding his fists together, he raises his arms and takes a heavy swing in my direction. I charge directly towards him, and just before his fists come together on either side of my face, I drop down, sliding between his legs. Leaping to my feet before his drug-induced haze alerts him to my presence behind him, I spin to face his back. With one of the greatest efforts of my life, I thrust the knife upwards at an angle, practically burying the hilt into his flesh. I twist my hand around the handle and yank it out, rotating it as I pull it from his back. He drops to his knees and falls to the floor, eyes wide from the blow.

It isn't until my dagger clatters to the floor that I realize how much I am shaking.

Slumping against the wall, I look at the mess around me. Blood splatters decorate the walls, chairs lie upturned, and the dwindling fire releases a few last puffs of crisp white smoke as it dies in the fireplace.

At least two of the men are still living, left by my hand to slowly bleed out. Unless a healer of exceptional ability finds them soon, they're not long for this world. The green man lies on his stomach, looking supremely shocked to be there, dying. One hand grips loosely around his throat, as if trying to stanch the bleeding. Unable to speak, he simply opens his mouth and closes it again in a comical imitation of a fish.

Closing my eyes, I think to pray. When I kill an animal for food or pelt, I thank the goddess for their life and for the gift I am receiving. For this? Well, I'm glad I'm still alive, but I'm not thanking anyone until the princess is found safe, and with me.

Digging into the green man's shirt, I pluck the button from within and hold it up to the light. It really is exquisite. The level of craftsmanship that the silversmith must have possessed! The crow's head is stunning, and the eye is set perfectly. The button is well worn - one side roughly polished from repeated fastenings. It's either old, or put on and off very frequently. Stuffing it into my coin purse, I stand and give one last look around the room. Snatching the money from the table and securing a piece of food or two, I leave the cottage and the men behind. It's time to find the princess. And I know where I want to begin my search.

*****

The old oak door cracks open half an inch, one tiny eye peeking through. A squeal of delight sounds from within and the door flies open, Enora's greeting a high pitched squeal of excitement.

"Uma! Look who it is!" She rushes me, wrapping her arms around my waist in a hug that wounds my already damaged ribs. I yelp a little, stepping back, and the overly worried look on her face crushes my soul to go along with the rest of my pain.

"No, no, it's fine," I apologize to her. "I'm sorry. I didn't mean to scare you and you didn't do anything wrong. I just.. Well, I've gotten myself a little beaten up here and there, and my ribs are bruised. It would have been a wonderful hug otherwise."

Uma slides into the doorway, looking even more ancient than before, if that's possible. Resting a hand on Enora's shoulder, she grins her toothless smile at me. "Looks like you've learned a few tough lessons in the past week." Her eyes travel up and down, collecting information of my injuries. "You look worse than me."

Laughing, she turns and steers Enora inside, beckoning me in. Enora hangs a kettle over the fire and settles onto the bed, eyes wide and fixed on me. "I'm sorry you're hurt..." Her voice trails off as she swallows a comment, eyes glued to my swollen and closed eye.

I smile at her as best I can.

Uma takes a seat nearby. "What brings you here, then?"

Simple and to the point. I always knew I liked Uma.

"I'm looking for someone. Tell me, have you or Andrew-" I smile down at Enora, trying to incorporate her into the conversation to show my trust - "or you.. Have any of you heard anything strange or alarming about one of the princesses?"

Enora shakes her head and Uma frowns. "Nothing more than usual. The same whirlings of a curse, how they're all becoming cold-hearted, empty souls."

"Mmm." I know the likelihood of the princess's kidnapping would not have made the local gossip circuit. Whomever is behind this wants everyone involved wiped out. If it were political or for ransom, there'd be a trail of breadcrumbs pointing the way.

"In that case.. What can you tell me about this?"

Pulling the button out from my purse, I place it gently into her withered palm. Her eyes fly open, wide with shock.

"Where did you get this?" She practically hisses at me, a distinct note of fear in her voice.

Ignoring her question, I press her for answers. "What do you know about this? Please, Uma, tell me."

Lifting her gaze to mine, she stares at me for a few minutes, breathing silently. Enora nervously looks between the two of us. "Uma? Are you alright?"

Uma gently waves away Enora's concerns, looking down at the button. Tracing her thumb along the decorative detail, she lets out a deep sigh. "Do you know anything about the man they call Corvus?"

"Of course not, Uma. Does this belong to him?"

"It does. Or at least, it did. No one has heard from him - or about him - in years." She closes her eyes for a second, and when she opens them, her eyes are fixed on me with a stare so intense, I begin to grow uncomfortable.

"You must be careful to whom you speak his name. But know this; you are far more involved in whatever you seek than you know. Corvus is now nothing more than a legend."

"But when he was alive? Who was he?" I cut her off, leaning forward in my impatience for the truth.

"The last time anyone heard of Corvus, he'd just helped your mother kill the last queen."

12

"Corvus... and my mother?"

"You realize, of course, that this is all conjecture. You and I both believe in your mother's innocence. But there is always some truth to legends, and your mother was at least involved in the time before the queen's death. Corvus was as well. Shrouded in mystery, Corvus was often heard about but never seen; at least, not by many. There were those who claimed to have seen him, but the fear that surrounds his name is real. It was not uncommon for people to have died in bloody ways, with the only thing left behind a button just like this one. And there was one placed over the queen's left eye when they found her."

"Then why is it that my mother was considered the murderer? Why was it not Corvus?"

Uma leans back in her chair, a sad look in her eyes. "The king feared magic more than anything. It was, perhaps, an unreasonable fear, but it was born of good reason. His first wife was one of those blessed with magic. After the birth of her daughter Helene, she went mad and used her magic for all sorts of insanity. The king tried to stop her, but in the end, he had her imprisoned and eventually divorced her. Three marriages more to foreign princesses, ten more daughters, and every time a wife began to assert herself or do something that made him uneasy, the king's fears crept in and doubt commanded his actions. Eventually, those wives were executed for treason. Pressured to produce a son, he took a final wife from the commoners, certain she could have no ulterior motives. She was a good person, and the two loved each other well. The king looked at her with all the light of the sun. She was beloved by the people, and a symbol of hope that the king had found his happiness. She bore him one last child, the youngest princess, and your mother attended her birth. When all was finished, the queen lay dead, not a mark on her body, but the midwives were slain, and your mother was found clutching the child to her chest behind a secret panel in the room.

"I believe your mother is innocent. I am certain in Corvus' guilt. Please, tread carefully. I do not know what awaits you."

She reaches forward and places the button back into my hand.

A soft whimper from Enora catches my attention and I can see the girl shivering slightly in fear. Knowing that I always feel better with action, I shrug out of the tattered remnants of the makeshift sling fashioned by the princess just the night before.

"Don't worry, Enora. I'll do my absolute best and be the safest I can be, but I need your help." Handing her the fabric, I nod towards her sewing items. "Can you make me a new one? Something that helps?"

Eyes shining brightly, she grins with enthusiasm. "Yes! Yes I can!"

Enora goes to sit at the table, a look of fierce concentration written across her brow. Uma stares at me, unmoving. Eventually she speaks, her voice pitched low and gentle. "I have seen enough to know that you have lived a hard life, but you have a kind soul."

Uncomfortable with the praise, I give her a grim smile, changing the subject quickly. "Uma, where can I find the village silversmith?"

"The only silversmith in Gormliath is the king's personal blacksmith. He has a forge at the base of the castle on the west side of the mountain."

"Thank you." There's a prolonged silence, before she stands, breathing deeply.

"Alright, young lady. Let's get you cleaned up. Your arm looks like it could use a little attention."

*****

Two hours later, I'm restlessly pacing around the room as Enora puts the finishing touches on a complicated but impressive sling for my arm. My sleeve is repaired, my chest bindings are re-wrapped as tightly as I can handle, and Enora is sewing furiously, pins tucked between her lips.

"Calm yourself! You'll wear a hole in your shoes from all that back and forth!" Uma growls at me crossly.

"It's near sundown." Trying and failing to keep the irritability out of my voice, I glance at Enora's work. Luckily, she is focused enough to miss my frustration and I sit, trying to give the guilt I feel about rushing her a larger hold in my emotions.

Searching for something to do, I test the bandage on my arm. Thankfully, the cut is long but not deep, and though one of Andrew's leather belts will never lose the marks of my teeth, the wound is now cleaned and bandaged well. The swelling on my face is calming after an hour of lying on the bed with a poultice of honey nettle resting over my eye and cheek. I hate feeling helpless, and the frequent visits outside to check the position of the sun in the sky has my anxiety ramping up.

"I'm finished!" Enora squeals as she holds up the new sling. It's made of rough burlap, but stitched together firmly. She stands and excitedly talks me through the design, mouth running at a speed I can barely follow. "Alright then, let's see!"

Navigating around my bandage, I gingerly shift into the sling, and Enora secures it with a leather tie at the top. The stiffness and soreness in my shoulder is immensely relieved and I beam at her in gratitude.

"Enora, you glorious creature!" I kiss both her cheeks and ruffle her hair. "Tell your brother hi for me."

Turning to Uma, I don't know what to say. So I settle on the only thing that feels appropriate now. "Thank you."

"You've no reason to thank me. But I hear you all the same. Now, go."

She nods towards the exit and I duck through the doorway into the crepuscular light, silently whispering prayers of protection over them.

Moving through the streets as quickly as I can to avoid suspicion, I come to the castle gate. Typically I'd veer to the right towards the stables. Today, I walk to the left and follow the worn dirt path along the base of the castle's thick stone walls.

I can smell my destination before I can see it. The unmistakably dirty smell of coal leads me until the warm orange glow from fires competes with the setting sun against the mountainside. A small wooden building sits here along the edge of the mountain, and as I turn the corner an ornate forge comes into view, sweeping stone carved into the side of the mountain as the castle looms high above us. One of the largest I've seen, boasting three separate forges with numerous anvils and grindstones being worked by a multitude of men. I am astounded by the bustle of activity, especially this late in the day. Shaking off the confusion, I formulate a quick plan in my head. Stepping back under the cover of the mountainside, I pull my hair tightly up again, tucking it firmly into place. Once satisfied, I grit my teeth. Cursing under my breath at the pain, I slip my arm from its sling, removing it and placing it in my hip satchel. Straightening my arm as best I can, I flex my wrists and roll my shoulder until I can assume a normal posture. With a deep breath, I step from cover and approach the nearest man who looks as if he has a moment to spare.

"Where can I find the lead man here? I'm looking for the royal blacksmith."

He pauses, sussing me out with a slow, critical evaluation. Apparently he judges me harmless, because he points with his chin towards a man standing on the far side of the forge, hammering at a red-hot sword with intimidating strength.

I approach cautiously, making mental notes of every detail in case I need them later. Waiting until he reaches for the bellows, I step in.

"Sir, I'm looking for the best sword maker in all of Gormliath. I was told you were the one to speak to."

His gruff reply is nothing more than a grunt, and I step in front of him, dangerously approaching the blazing hot blade.

"I am here to hire your skill, and I won't take no for an answer." Holding out the bag of coins I stole from the assassins at the cottage in the glen, I nod my head towards the small building, judging this to be the forgemaster's quarters. "Perhaps we can discuss this in private. It is of a... confidential nature."

His eyes travel to the coin purse and then to my eyes. I stare him down, unintimidated. Judging by the activity here, I can tell the forge is busy. With what, I'm not sure, but I hardly believe a country like Gormliath is working this hard on weaponry and defensive items on a typical day. Someone is up to something, and the sinister air of the kingdom's secrets churns in my head.

The forgemaster finally consents, calling over another worker to finish the sword in his hand, then walks to the entrance of his quarters.

"Come in." His voice is gruff, and he appears to be a man of few words. Better for me, to be honest.

We step inside and he leans against the table in the middle of the room. "Let's see that gold, then."

I smirk at him, fingers toying with the leather thong holding the coin pouch closed. "What makes you think it is gold, and not silver?"

"'Cause no lass with an injured arm would come in here and waste my time for silver, expecting to get out alive. So then. Let's see that gold."

I smile at him. Of course he is no fool. He saw through me on both fronts immediately. Shrugging, I toss him the pouch, keeping the throw just a little short. As he leans forward to reach for it, I slide my dagger from under my arm and slip behind him, pressing the knife to his throat, wrapping my injured arm as tightly as I can around his waist.

"Don't. Fucking. Move."

I can feel his anger and embarrassment at being had, but he's not a stupid man. He stands still as I take the coin purse back and instead, pull out the button and hold it up in front of his eyes.

"Does this look familiar?"

A subtle clench of his abdominal muscles against my arm tells me all I need to know; and I can see in his neck just above the knife point that his pulse grows stronger as his heart rate quickens. Not waiting for an answer, I continue. "I see. Let's put it this way, then. Tell me who you made this for and where I can find him, and I might let you go."

A small strangled sound gurgles inside his throat, but he clears it and emits a bitter laugh. "You're a foolish girl. One shout from me, and these men will descend upon this building and skin you alive. After they have their fun with you, of course."

"You're positively adorable if you think I won't have cut out your vocal cords before you can take even a breath louder than this." Pressing the point of my knife deeper into his skin I can feel him swallow, the movement causing the dagger to nick his skin. "Aww, now see? You're hurting yourself now. Maybe you do want to die."

"N... no." The word is barely a whisper and I can practically feel his pride evaporating as the need for self-preservation wins out.

"Then I suggest you tell me, now. I'm growing tired of this game, and you're not the only one I can get information out of." I turn him ever so slightly so he and I share a view of a woman's bonnet sitting nearby on the table. "I'm sure she could help..."

"It wasn't me." He almost laughs, the way the words come out. "My father made them. You're awfully stupid if you think I'm old enough to have crafted those."

Fuck! I hadn't considered this in all of my careful consideration and in my self-anger, I can feel the blade sink deeper into his throat. I freeze, knowing even a centimeter more and I might kill him or eliminate his ability to speak - and the truth is, I need this lead. *Not that he needs to know that.*

My moment of accidental anger bears fruit, however. The man yelps a bit, and begins to vibrate against me in fear. "Wait! I'll tell you. I don't know who he was, but I was a boy and my father took me with him. We delivered them to a house in the woods, not far from here. There was a man who lived there. I.. I can draw you a map."

"A map won't be necessary. Just tell me what I need to know." I hiss into his ear, and he quickly recounts the details. Down the mountain, into the woods, past the split rowan tree, beyond the waterfall. Less than quarter hour's walk.

"There's a good boy. Now. I'm going to leave, and you're going to count to thirty before you return to the forge. In that time," I tap against the side of his neck with the blade, "I should consider it wise to clean yourself up, lest your men think less of you. Beaten by a girl. Why, I can already imagine the gossip!" A giggle escapes my lips, making me think I must sound quite mad. "I thank thee for your services, good sir. Have a lovely evening." With a humiliating kiss to the side of his face, I push him away from me and slip out the back window of his cottage, racing down the hillside into the encroaching darkness.

13

Racing against the sunset, I rush into the woods, searching the dim light for a split rowan tree. Once I see it I pick up my pace, following the slowly growing sound of rushing water. As the waterfall comes into view I push myself faster, legs screaming in protest. At one point I backtrack, wondering if I've lost the trail, but finally a small circular hut with a tall thatched roof comes into view. The windows are dark, and no smoke spirals from the chimney. Hoping no one is home, I skid to a stop and slowly creep closer, keeping low to the ground.

Gently feeling the walls on either side of the chimney, I feel no residual warmth. Doesn't seem like anyone has lit a fire any time soon, and I can hear nothing from inside, so I peek into one of the windows. There's no one here, but it is obviously still inhabited. Determined to find answers, I hop into one of the windows and slip inside.

My eyes adjusting to the darkness inside, I quickly take in the space. The room is simple enough, but immediately I can tell that something seems off. The bed is roughly put together, but the mattress looks exceptionally plush. Every cooking implement looks new, barely worn or blackened by soot and flame. A bundle of perfectly formed candles as thick as my wrist lay in a nearby basket, with bunches of fresh fruit and salted meats hanging from racks above the table. Peering into the fireplace, I sift my fingers through the ash; bits of paper torn and burned flutter around the edges. Wishing desperately for more light, I look longingly again at the candles, but I don't chance lighting one. I must leave things exactly as I've left them, and any light could be seen from the outside, alerting someone to my presence here.

The chest nearby sits cracked open by just a hair, the latch loosely closed. The only item in the cottage that appears old, my interest is immediately piqued. This is special, for some reason. This holds value. In a place where someone has enough income to have expensive new items in their home, why hang on to something tattered and worn, with a broken hinge like this?

Pulling the latch loose with a gentle touch, I slowly lift the lid. A woolen blanket sits on top, and a few old tomes lay beneath them. Their topics are bizarre, but not so alarming; at least until I see a glimmer on the cover of the lowest book. Lifting the massive volume in my hands, I can't help but gasp. An old and weathered grimoire rests in my hands and with a lurch in my stomach, I find I can no longer ignore all the signs; whatever all this is, it's magic, and I feel utterly powerless against it.

Thumbing through the pages, my nausea deepens. This is old magic, and dark. No healing spells or ways to conjure water; this book is designed for death and destruction.

Tucking it back neatly into the trunk, there is one last item. A smooth wooden box of impeccable craftsmanship and design. A black horse is carved into the lid, graceful and beautiful mid-stride. I run my fingers over it, feeling a strange sense of calling to the container and its contents. Removing it from the chest, I rest it across my knees and slide my fingers into the grooves along the front, lifting the lid to look inside.

"Mama!" The whisper slips past my lips in a gasp, a shock of fear and hurt and confusion and anger flashing through my veins in a surge of bitter adrenaline. Glinting back at me are the white crystal, emerald, and bloodstone of my mother's dagger, embedded into the hilt of her weapon in their perfect trifecta. The long, perfectly even blade is exactly as I remember it, and I can practically feel her presence.

As the fog in my brain clears and my thoughts gather, question after question tumble through my brain. Why is her dagger here? Is she still alive? Who is this Corvus person? Did she work with him? Did my mother truly kill the queen? Or even.. Is it possible that my mother is the mysterious Corvus?

I lift the dagger in my hands, running the tips of my fingers along the edges of the blade. Turning it back and forth, I balance the weight, memorizing the feel of it. The last time I held this I was a girl of eight and the blade took up considerably more space in my palm. Touching the jewels on the hilt, a flood of memories fills my mind, overwhelming my senses. Images fly through my head in rapid-fire succession, a thousand memories rolling by like spilled marbles in a child's game.

Rocking back on my heels, I clutch the weapon to me, and I sense a small tear sliding down my cheek. Choking back a sob, I can feel the blade sharp against my palms as I grasp it tightly in my hand. But I don't care. I cannot care. I feel broken in ways I cannot imagine.

Collecting myself and my emotions, I master a calm facade inside and out. Wiping the blade clean on my clothes, I make to return it to its case, but a small piece of paper tucked into the edge of the box catches my attention.

Curious, I pull out the folded parchment and open it, desperately trying to make out the words in the darkness.

"Kill the queen and the child. Ensure the healer is to blame. We meet at midnight."

I barely have the time to finish reading when a sound from outside the door catches my attention. Someone is here! Alarmed, I tuck the note back into the box, slip the dagger into its place and put everything back as quickly as possible. Barely closing the lid to the chest, I hop through the back window again and slip out just as the door opens.

Back against the wall, I silence my breathing as much as I can. Terrified at both the newly acquired knowledge and at the closeness of being caught, I close my eyes and listen keenly to the sounds coming from the window above me.

The door shuts roughly, and I hear a man's voice grunt softly with the effort. A few swishes of fabric, and then the sound of a heavy cloak falling over the back of a chair. I can make out the sound of a flint stone being struck, the soft fizzing of a newly lit flame, and the earthy aroma of a peat fire permeates the cabin not long after.

After some sounds of water and a metal scraping I assume to be a kettle slung over the iron hook above the fire, the man settles into a chair with a thud. He groans to himself, and I wrack my brain for details. Mentally assembling the room in my mind's eye, I remember the chair facing away from the window, and desperately wanting a glimpse, I decide to risk it. Slowly turning and pushing onto my knees, I rise just enough to peer in through the corner of the window. A man's back is to me, greasy dark hair slicked back in sweat. He rubs some water roughly over his face, yawning in an undignified fashion. A heavy wool cloak sits behind him, resting on the chair and I recognize the intricate buttons with the emerald eyes. That's it, then. This is Corvus. Same as it was 22 years ago. The blacksmith didn't even try to sell me false information. Almost laughable, I secretly thank him for his cowardice; I'll not mock any win I can get these days.

Eventually, Corvus turns to the side and the temperature in my body soars and plummets within the span of a half-second. A face far too familiar sits before me, calmly rubbing the soles of his feet as if his day didn't include a kidnapping and attempted murder. Sam.

Ducking back below the window, I feel a sudden sense of panic. I have to get away, fast. To think that someone as kind and, well, stupid as Sam could be Corvus! Afraid of what evils he is capable of, I creep towards the tree line, sheltering myself in the darkness that has now fallen firmly over the land.

Sam, sweet Sam! How could he be Corvus? And yet it makes such sense. Hiding in plain sight for so many years, laying low with a respectable position as the stablemaster, secretly working for someone all along. Thinking of the note I found, I feel more certain than ever that any momentary doubts as to the innocence of my mother are fully vanquished. She was framed, plain and simple, and that Corvus, er, Sam... was the murderer.

These thoughts swirl through my head as I move swiftly back to the waterfall, trying to maintain silence in my movements. Once the sound of water violently crashing down the mountainside fills my ears, I take off at a sprint, racing back towards the castle.

Who could Sam have been working for? And who is Sam working for now? Thinking back to the blacksmith, I remind myself that many years have gone by since then. Now in his mid forties, if I had to guess, Sam would have been a young man then, but a man all the same. Any loyalties he may have had twenty-two years ago could have since changed.

A sudden sense of desperation fills me; thinking of the look of terror in her eyes as she spoke of the night, the half-waking dreams, missing persons posters, and the townspeople's voices echoing the word 'curse' over and over again in my ears. Whatever she was captured for, I know in my gut they are connected, and I know that the darkness tonight will bring events with consequences that will last for all the ages. Every answer I can find now is crucial, and I make my way for the only other place I know Sam to inhabit.

Rounding the bottom of the mountain, I sprint into the stables, running for the stall where Sam keeps his things. Pulling open the gate, I spot Ewan, curled up in the straw, munching on a piece of bread and playing with a small doll made of dried corn husks.

"Oh!" Surprise evident on my face, I try to make light of what I'm doing. Now I understand why Ewan is always here. Sam gives him a place to stay out of the elements, and Ewan guards Sam's secrets - whether he knows it or not.

"There you are!" Shifting my expression to one of relief and satisfaction, I give the boy a wide grin. "I've been looking for you!" I settle into the hay next to him and quickly pull a coin from the pouch at my waist. Without him seeing, I tuck it into my palm, held flat by the base of my fingers.

"Goodness... Ewan, when was the last time you took a bath! Why, you're positively filthy! What's this here, stuck behind your ear?" I flick my wrist behind him, touching the back of his ear gently, and return with the coin in my fingertips. With a giggle, I hand it to him, laughing at the wide eyes and enchanted delight written plain on his face.

"Go on, then. Buy yourself something nice."

He turns a shocked face to me, full of disbelief at my generosity. "Yes, you! I'll stay here for just a few moments, so go get a treat and come right back!"

The smile on his face is full and bright and giddy, and he nods, shakes my hands enthusiastically, and races out the door.

As soon as I'm certain he is gone, I throw myself into searching through every nook and cranny of the stall. No horse is housed here, and I'm certain I know why. I feel along the ground under the hay, searching desperately for anything that feels out of place. Suddenly, my hand makes contact with something rough and cold, and I realize I'm gripping a handle of some sort. Shoving the hay out of the way, I pull back to reveal a door in the floor, a large iron bar forming a sort of crude handle. Pulling on it, a few planks shift and I lift it up to reveal a small cubby built into the ground.

Inside are only a few items; a leather bound book, a pair of leather gloves, and a large, ornate brass key. Picking up the book, I look inside. A correspondence, it appears, with two distinct handwritings but written in a cipher. To my eyes, it's absolute gibberish. Frustrated, I flip the pages quickly to scan for anything that appears different from the rest. There, on the last page, is a map of some sort. I study it, twisting it until I recognize any features, as this map contains no words and is all sketched roughly in the same thick black charcoal. On a third rotation, I recognize the stables, then the forge, then the castle... ticking off locations I'm familiar with, I find a small stream that flows by the castle's outer walls further east from the stables. Where the stream and the castle meet, a large X. Quickly placing the book and the gloves back into the hole, I slip the key into my pocket and slide the cover back over, quickly rearranging the hay as best I can, sitting back comfortably against the wall again.

Impatiently waiting another minute, I silently apologize to Ewan for breaking my promise, but slip out the door to follow the map now in my mind.

It doesn't take me long to locate the stream, but the entrance to the castle is nowhere to be seen. Stumbling along the banks of the small creek, I search desperately for the place where the wall and water meet, but it seems to stretch on forever. Panic begins to set in as I keep the pace, anxious and uncertain if I've perhaps missed the entrance, my foot slips on a rock and I go down, hard. Wincing with pain, I curse under my breath, staring at the castle wall. Frustration and anger setting in, I stand and turn in the opposite direction, thinking I should retrace my steps.. and then, I see it. A small trickle of water pulling away from the main stream, running into the castle wall, obscured from my previous view by one of many bushes growing along the base of the castle walls. Hesitantly approaching it, I see not a gate, or a door, but... a hole. A narrow pit built into the side of the wall, water trickling down into it. It's wide enough, but not by much, murky darkness swallowing up any end to the passage in sight.

This is a hopelessly stupid thing to do.

Holding my breath, I jump down into the hole.

14

The inside of my already injured palms scrape against the stone walls as I slide downwards, cushioned only by the moss growing on the damp walls. Skidding down, I'm gathering speed when with a jolt my feet slam into the ground, my boots filling with water.

Sucking in a breath, I freeze, hoping that my entrance doesn't attract unwanted attention. Hearing nothing, I let out my air and open my eyes, observing my surroundings.

A long, dark tunnel stretches out before me, sporadic torches flickering as far as I can see. Torches are bad. Torches mean I can see, but they also mean someone has been here, and most likely that someone else is expected.

Sliding my knife out from under my arm, I adjust my stance and slowly begin to walk forward.

Every single step echoes broadly, water sloshing beneath my feet. I study the ground, deciding it best to walk cautiously along the stones than to continue to make so much noise. My pace slows considerably, but the slick lichen-covered rocks provide a much welcome silence to my footfalls.

Creeping along at a snail's pace to ensure I don't lose my balance, the torches eventually stop, and I stare into a void of blackness, threatening to swallow me whole. I look back over my shoulder, seeing no other way to have gone. With a gulp of fear, I face the darkness once more, and step into the abyss.

Suddenly it is unnaturally cold. If I could see, I'm sure I would watch little clouds of air puffing in front of my face with each shaky breath. An oppressive atmosphere weighs down around me and the darkness feels alive. Now that the use of magic in all of this has been confirmed, I find myself trembling with fear. Drawing in a slow and shaky breath, I talk myself through what I know.

I possess no magical qualities, nor am I resistant to magic. If I am to solve these mysteries so apparently intertwined, I need to rely on who I am and what I can do. I'm fast, I'm clever, and I can keep in cover well, concealing my whereabouts. If I rely on my gifts, the ones hard earned by a life of anger and pain, I may just get out of here alive.

My confidence bolstered, a tiny hint of warmth tingles through the ends of my fingers, and I press on into the darkness. Reaching my hands out in front of me, I walk slowly, unable to see even two inches in front of my face.

Matching my breathing with my steps, I count my paces. Twenty-one, twenty-two, twenty-three... just when it feels that I'll end my days trapped in this never-ending darkness, the tips of my fingers press into something solid.

Anxiously feeling around, my touch finds long planks of wood, metal hinges, and a curved stone doorframe.

Searching for the handle, I press down on the latch, and push.

A slight groaning noise meets my efforts, but the door doesn't open. Engaging the handle, I pull this time, straining with the efforts of shifting this massively heavy door. But still the door doesn't move.

Wiping an arm across my face to clear the beads of sweat dappling across my brow, I stop and think. Reaching another hand out, I locate the handle once more, but feel along the metal framing surrounding the door's latch. Fingers dancing across the cold wet metal as slowly as I can make them, I hold my breath in concentration. There, two centimeters to the left, is a small notch in the metal, a perpendicular slot made perfectly for a key.

The key! Thrusting my fingers into my hip pouch, I sift through coins until the lattice work of the keyhead brushes against my thumb and I grasp it tightly between my fingers. Guiding the key with both hands, I carefully fit it into the slot, pushing until I hear a click. With a gentle turn, the lock disengages, and the door shifts softly on its hinges. Pocketing the key once more, I grasp the handle, and push it open.

The room beyond the door is still swallowed in darkness, but a source of light shines down on me. I can see the faint outline of a wide, sweeping staircase rising before me, a light set somewhere along its path. With a deep breath, I begin my ascent.

The staircase is dizzyingly long, winding incessantly in an upward spiral. How long have I been climbing? I am completely disoriented, unsure of where I am. Feeling as if I must be stories above ground by now, my steps quicken, desperate to end this crushing feeling that I'm caught in a never-ending maze.

On and on I climb until at last the stairs even out onto a landing. A plush velvet chair with finely carved mahogany sits just outside a door, a burning candle in a brass holder resting on a small table nearby. Cautiously approaching, I rest my hand on the seat of the chair. It's still warm; someone was just here. Pressing my ear against the door, I can hear movement and the voices of many on the other side. Laying flat on the floor, I peer through the crack just under the door. Numerous soft slippered feet move to and fro, skirts of every color swirling around ankles as women giggle and chat. The words I can make out are vain, prideful boasts of tiny waists or luscious red lips, competing even with each other.

"Oh, Isabell, your gown is stunning. Truly. I'm sure there are some noblemen out there who prefer their women in dresses of pea-green. It's such a fetching shade." Sarcasm drips from the closest voice, mocking one of the other women.

"This gown was custom made by Geraldine Riversa, which is more than I can say for yours. Do you like being the second to youngest, passing off your dresses to the mender so they can be altered to fit your figure? All those extra panels. Why, it's a waste! If you weren't so fat, father wouldn't have to spend so much money on alterations for your gowns!"

A loud voice cuts through the room, deep and powerful. "If father wasn't such an imbecile, we wouldn't be a kingdom with embarrassingly empty coffers and could afford to buy as many dresses for Annabell as she wanted." The room stills at her words, a sign of deference easily earned. "Don't listen to her, cherub. She's only jealous of your figure."

"Thank you, Helene."

Helene, Annabell, Isabell... I know these names. These are the princesses, without a doubt. Obviously preparing for some sort of event, I try to recall the details of Meg's dream to me. She spoke of dancing and feasting, and I wonder if this is what she referred to. Goosebumps ripple across the back of my neck.

There's a long drawn-out pause, and then Helene speaks again. "We have something to celebrate tonight, sisters. Our sweet little Meg has come back to the fold once more." There's absolutely nothing in the tone of her voice that makes me believe she finds Meg sweet at all, but there's an appropriate murmuring of appreciation at her words. "To think she was so lost, failing to fulfill her destiny. We shall toast to her safe return at the banquet tonight."

"Thank you, sister." It's Meg's voice, of this I am certain. But she sounds stiff and formal, empty and void of the ebullient woman I know. *At least she is alive!* A deep rush of relief courses through my body.

"There's a good girl." Helene's voice is smug and mocking, and I wish to break down the door and embed my fist into her face. My thoughts race and I piece together the information I know. Helene is behind all of this, I'm sure of it. But... why?

There is a loud scraping noise, like a chair being pushed across the floor, and her commanding voice rings out once more. "This is an important night for us, sisters. The moon is full, and the Midnight Kingdom will be at its strongest. Let us renew our souls!"

I can hear three light taps, and then a sound that vibrates all through the floor echoes all around me. Jumping up, I look around terrified, but nothing has changed on my end. Scuffles of feet across smooth wooden floors and then the giggles and whispers disappear, leaving silence on the other side of the door.

Where did they go? What happened? As my thoughts race, I am

pulled to reality by the sound of a door far behind me opening. Perhaps Corvus is coming, or another; but I cannot risk finding out. Throwing caution to the wind, I seize the latch on the door and try to force it open. It doesn't budge, so I pull the key out once again and slip it into the lock. With a quick turn of my wrist, I open the door and step inside, closing the door behind me.

A massive room extends before me, ornate silver sconces on the walls casting it in a bright orange glow. Large beds with expansive red canopies line each wall, towering wardrobes positioned between each one. Nightgowns and bed slippers are tossed haphazardly about, the room in a general state of disarray. Drawers and armoire doors remain open, and small cups of makeup powders sit on tables around the room, brushes rolling back and forth in evidence of a quick exit. The sisters have left in a hurry, with no regard to the state of the chamber.

A strange noise from the end of the room catches my attention, the same rumbling shaking the ground beneath my feet. At the end of a row of beds, I can see a large cavern set into the floor. I race towards it as a final bed slowly rises up from within the floor, covering a staircase that is disappearing beneath it.

Sure that the princesses have somehow made their exit through this bizarre outlet, I race towards the quickly disappearing passage, sliding on my hip through the narrow gap just as the base of the bed shifts into place, sealing off the bedroom above.

I thud down a set of stairs, each drop sending a splinter of hurt through my side as I bite my lip to keep from crying out in pain. Landing squarely on my bottom, I flop unceremoniously onto the ground. Groaning under my breath and massaging my hip, I glare up at the steps I've just tumbled down, a grandiose staircase of black marble that deposited me in front of the largest gate I have ever seen in my entire life. Rich iron reaches in detailed scrollwork thirty feet into the air, each door wider than my arm span by far. Looking to my right and left, there is nothing but oppressive darkness in either direction.

Pacing to the gate, I hesitantly reach out and touch it. No shock, no pain, no transfiguration; it appears to be no magical substance. Coming closer, I peer through the gate, and can just make out the final flutters of dresses disappearing ahead.

Grasping the metal firmly, I yank at the door with all my might, and it slowly opens just enough for me to step through to the other side.

The environment changes in an instant. A strange, ethereal sight greets me, where impenetrable darkness is battled by a subtle glimmer as otherworldly plants glow in dull greens, purples, and blues. Tiny fireflies flit through the air, looking almost like miniature moving stars. A path is worn into the ground at my feet, but my still-wet boots crunch noisily against the gravel with every cautious step. Slipping my boots off, the gravel muffles well now, and I move silently through the darkness.

Far beyond me in the distance I can hear echoes of soft laughter and squeals of delight, enthusiasm for their destination apparent in their voices.

Continuing on, the bizarre landscape rounds a bend and when I make the turn, a gasp slips past my lips, echoing through the cavernous world.

A forest lays before me, made up of what can only be described as pure, sterling silver. Frigidly cold air lends the impression of winter and gleaming trees reflect a pearlescent glow back to me, casting the light of a moon that is somehow pitched high in the sky. Every branch is magnificent and strong, stretching their tendrils towards the sky.

The whole world set in vivid white, I pace along the path through this hauntingly beautiful forest, trying to keep my awe in check. This is still dark magic, and I can assume that the stunning environment is meant to distract from something more sinister.

Picking up the pace, I keep to the side of the path and run as much as I can through the silver forest, hoping to close the distance somewhat between the princesses and me. But my pace once again slows as the trees shift from silver into gold, glittering now under a brightly shining star. Fragile golden leaves decorate sturdy golden branches, the whole world a sickly orange glow under the intensity of the star's reflection. Even more stunning and yet more discomforting, the golden forest fills me with unease and a sweltering heat settles over my skin. Desperate for water, I push on, the heavy air and golden glow seeming to close in on me from all sides.

No longer able to hear any voices, I push on, sweat trickling in thick droplets down the sides of my face.

And then at once, the gold shifts and I skid to a stop, a peculiar feeling in my chest. The air suddenly thins, the heat disappears, and I'm standing in the middle of a forest of diamonds.

A thousand faces reflect back at me, my own bewildered expression on each of them as countless diamonds hang from tree branches. The trees themselves glitter under a pure white light, and the glinting reflections are almost too bright to view.

Gasping for breath as I walk along, what could be seen as beautiful to some feels sharp and cutting to me, each gemstone looking like a tiny dagger dangling from a tree branch. The mirror-like forest is disorienting, and if not for the path I'm sure I could be lost within these trees forever.

When it feels as if my oxygen is nearing its end, the forest clears, and I stumble out onto what can only be described as a beach. Silver sand rests beneath my toes, and before me lies a massive lake with water as black as ebony glass. Far across the lake, a deep purple sky frames a towering castle that looks to be made of shadows, lights dancing in windows crawling ten stories high. Set into the highest tower rises a vivid crystal, catching both a beam of blue-white light shining brighter than I've ever seen, and a stream of something thick and black, a void that seems to flow directly into the crystal's heart.

Twelve small boats are midway through their journey across the lake, soft ripples left in their wake as oars dip into the water. My eyes glancing all around, I find that no more boats remain.

Knowing that jumping into an unfamiliar lake in a magical land could mean certain death, I search and find a small rock. Tossing it into the water... if we can call it that ... it bobs and sinks appropriately, no fizzing or bubbles from acid devouring the substance whole. Deciding that a rock might be too hearty, I pluck a nearby flower, dipping the delicate flowers into the lake's murky depths. Petals still intact, I hold my breath and gently step into the water.

Nothing happens. Satisfied, I wade into the water until my thighs are submerged. Sensing no more trouble, I dive under the water and take off at a lightning pace swimming after the boats towards the castle in the center of the lake.

The substance in the lake is thicker than water, and it isn't long before my muscles are wearying with the effort. Pausing to rest, I search the waterline for the boats and find them pulled upon the distant shore, each princess being escorted by a partner. They coo and flirt, swatting at their companions with coquettish advances, but one woman moves as if possessed. She is wooden, slow, and automatic, devoid of any real personality. Rising to the top of the bank I can see her more clearly, and the sight of unmistakable raven ringlets that flow to her waist makes my blood run cold. Meg.

The voice inside my head screams her name, and I kick forward once more, racing towards her with every stroke. The castle grows closer and though my lungs are screaming and muscles protesting, threatening to give out, I push harder. The shore looms large, and I know I'm close. Yes! With one final push, I reach my fingers out, desperate for the feel of sand beneath my touch... when something slimy and strong coils around my ankle and tugs down hard, pulling me beneath the surface of the lake and down into the depths of darkness.

15

I open my mouth to scream, the syrupy black liquid crawling down my throat, trying to fill my lungs. Snapping my mouth shut, I wrestle my knife out from underneath my arm and slash at whatever has me in its snares. Quick slashes do nothing to lessen the grip on my ankle, so pausing my movements for a second, I gather my strength and stab downward with all of the strength I have left. A sickening scream sends a shockwave of ripples through the lake and I am thrust backwards towards the surface, my body limp like seaweed floating in the ocean. Breaking the surface, I gasp for breath, eyes bulging from my skull as I attempt to fill my lungs with air once more.

Kicking with all my might for the shore, I glance behind me in terror, hoping to avoid more of what just tried to end my life. Goddess be praised, with my next stroke I thrash into the sand and grapple with frigid fingers as I scramble up upon the shore, terrified, sopping wet, and shivering.

This place is madness! I pull back my pant leg and see a sickly purple bruise wrapped in layers around my ankle that oozes a green, sap-like substance. It burns and my hands shake as I do my best to clear the contamination from the wound. Once I'm certain I can walk, I rise to unsteady feet and brush the sand off of my clothes and skin.

One thing's for certain. When all of this is said and done, I'm buying myself new clothes. And a barrel of mead. Yes. Mead.

Gritting my teeth against the innumerable aches, pains, and injuries

I sport, I take off up the shoreline, racing towards the castle, my dagger clutched tightly in my hand.

As I near the massive building, I duck behind a low wall and observe what I can. A large banquet hall is the centerpiece of the main floor, light pouring out from a multitude of windows onto perfectly manicured gardens. Within the room a host of people spin and twirl on the dancefloor, all dressed in excessively ornate attire and masks that cover their faces. An orchestra provides lively music, and a long table set with food more decadent than I've ever seen lines one of the lengthy exterior walls.

In any other situation, this would look like nothing more than another lavish party hosted by royals with unlimited budget and even less concern for the welfare of their constituents. But I know better, and I creep closer, eventually ducking into the open window of a dark hallway in close proximity to the banquet hall. I creep along, four paces in when a door on my left opens and a servant steps out, empty goblets of wine perched precariously on a gilded silver tray. He gasps at the sight of me, the glasses tipping over, and I dart forward just in time to keep the tray and goblets from clattering to the ground. Sensing the opportunity before me, I smile at him and step closer, cornering him against the wall. Taking the tray from his trembling hands, I lean down and whisper in his ear.

"Don't take this personally, darling." With the butt end of my dagger, I knock him out and drag him into the dark corner of the hall. Donning his clothes and mask, I ring as much moisture from my hair as I can and knot it up on the back of my head. Finishing with his shoes, I stand and pick up the tray again, pushing through the door and into the party.

Smiling demurely, I quickly observe the behaviors and posture of nearby servants and adopt their mannerisms. Gliding through the room, I keep my tray presented openly and guests set their empty glasses on my tray as I walk through the room.

Confused as to the number of people in this underground, magical party, I make a quick circuit of the room observing the crowd. Faces all obscured, I don't recognize anyone nor can I identify any person's face. Once my tray is full, I duck into cover behind a massive potted spray fern, setting the tray aside. From my new vantage point, I take an even longer look around the room, eyes moving past the dancers and drinkers to the head table.

An elegant woman with blonde hair piled high above her head sits in a towering throne-like chair in the middle. She leans back in her seat, a calculating eye scanning the room with a hawk-like nature. A deeply vivid dress of crimson sits primly upon her shoulders with an excessively low-cut neckline broadcasting her apparent sense of self-importance. A thick banded choker decorates her neck, with a diamond the size of my eye dangling from its center.

Next to her, a crow stands on the table, little beady eyes focused on the woman almost as if it worships her as she idly strokes a finger up and down its back.

Drawing my eyes away from her, I look through the crowd for Meg, wondering if I can pick her out from the whirling faces before me.

Closing my eyes, I recall the image in my mind of her disembarking the boat and lighting up the hillside, honing in on the subtle rose-pink sheen of her dress. My eyes fly open and I search for the color in the crowd.

I look everywhere, but the dancers move too quickly, until all of a sudden a pairing flies by just before me, skirting along the outside of the dancers' circle. The man's back to me, he spins her in a dramatic fashion, jet-black curls lifting from her shoulders as she turns in his arms. My heart nearly stops in my chest, the view before me slowing to a crawl as the scene unfolds in slow motion.

Meg's body moves past me, inches from my hiding spot behind the palm. Her dancing posture is impeccable, easy and free but with enough strength thrumming through her limbs to maintain a perfect frame. A broad, vivid smile sparkles beneath the mask that covers half of her face. All her movements are automatic, scripted, like a puppet on a string. Oh, how joyous she would look... if it weren't for her eyes.

Set back from the beaded edges in the mask, her eyes are wide, terrified, and in one corner, a small tear glimmers.

For a split second our eyes meet directly and I can see a flash of recognition and a burst of real, genuine, fear.

Spinning past, time resolves its rapid march and she twirls away with her partner, bustling along in the violent speed of the dance.

My mouth is dry, my heart is racing, and I want nothing more than to break from my cover, run to her, and pull her into my arms, whisking her away from all of this. But I know that beneath the terror in her eyes, something has control over her, and I'm afraid of what might happen if I break its grip before I understand the problem. With no clues and no understanding of what I'm up against, a helpless feeling begins to claw at my insides. Grasping at straws, I search my mind for what I know.

My eyes naturally drift back to the woman at the front, whom I can only assume is Helene. Her eyes are settled on Meg, following her around the room as the dance picks up speed. The intensity with which Helene stares her down makes my stomach curdle. The crow on the table with her cocks its head, blinks twice, and then takes off, slipping out the nearest window.

A new turn of fury rushes through my veins as I watch her sit there with her superior, lordly attitude. I clench my fists, glaring at her, as she rises from her seat. The music stops instantly and the dancers still as if the world revolves around her every whim and movement.

With every pair of eyes focused on her, she preens and beams at the crowd with a smile that stretches far too widely across her red painted cheeks.

"Good evening, everyone!"

The crowd mimics her greeting with enthusiasm, goblets raised in the air with gusto.

"I am so pleased to have you here. For these sacred hours we share together tonight, we laugh, we dine, and we dance. But once we leave here this evening, the work begins. My father's illness is progressing steadily. In less than two months' time, I shall be crowned Queen, and the Kingdom of Gormliath will enter into a new era!"

Cheers and bellows of support ripple through the crowd, drowning out the thoughts in my head as I digest the words she tosses to the people.

"We will rise again in glory and re-take our rightful place as the crown jewel in the seven sacred kingdoms. I will open our borders and we will march out into the world, bending the knees of all who refuse to bow to our greatness."

Another round of cheers soars to the ceiling, quieting quickly as her face crumbles almost comically into an expression of elaborate sorrow.

"My mother always said that magic was a gift from the gods. She knew that it was a gift, given to the special few meant to lead. She knew that to suppress magic only makes it stronger, and to ignore it only makes it louder. With magic once again, Gormliath will be free. No more will those with magic be murdered in the streets, executed by the soldiers of a weak and worthless king. No more will those with magic be subjected to living in the shadows, fearing for their lives. No more will our great kingdom be seen as the laughingstock of the empire, a fearful nation too keen to lick our wounds than to fight back. We will rise again, and we will be great!"

Her speech is rousing, yes. There is a level of pride that I can feel surging up from within me, a desire to fully imbue myself with the passion in her words. It snakes its way through my veins, a sharp, fiery heat beginning in my toes and climbing its way up into my body.

Staring at her, I find myself unable to look away. Helene is beautiful. Her leadership is obvious. And her dedication to her people is true! The more the creeping feeling of white-hot pins and needles worms its way through my veins, the stronger my belief in Helene grows. *Meg, sweet Meg... she must have been mistaken. I'll have to talk to her, to set her right. This is all so good!*

A soft, wet feeling tickles my toes, and I look down; a puddle of wine is soaking through my slipper. I must have upended a glass from my tray, spilling the last of its contents onto the floor. My shoe is already soaked through and stained with deep purple; my focus so intense on the words of my gorgeous future queen that I had no notice of the puddle at my feet. Reaching out, I touch the contents pooling on the floor, feeling another surge in my fingers of admiration and love for Helene and this place. Closing my eyes in utter bliss, I lick the wine droplets from the tips of my fingers.

Unlike anything I have ever tasted, the wine is sweet and almost brutal with how heavy its weight feels in my mouth. It coats the inside of my cheek and I run my tongue along it, yearning to capture more of the heavenly bouquet.

Fingers flying to the ground once more, I rub my hands through the wine, pulling them up to lick them dry. I cannot get enough. This is better than any mead or ale I've ever tasted.

Helene's voice trickles over the crowd once more and my head snaps up, eager to hear more of her fair voice. I scramble through the puddle on my knees, legs flushing with heat, to a new vantage point just beyond the fern, staring deeply into her vivid blue eyes.

"So now, my friends, eat, drink, and dance all the troubles away. For tomorrow, the real work begins. You will take your rightful place back in society and the seeds of revolution will be sewn. Let us celebrate!"

My head feels delightfully vacant, the room seeming to spin in a slow-motion menagerie. I observe the room with a giddy delight, enamored with the people around me. Helene now seated once more in her hawk's nest overseeing the festivities, the party takes a turn. The music slows to a sensual melody and the lights dim as servants rush to snuff out the massive candelabras on the dining and banquet tables. There is a new level of freedom for the guests as they chase the high that floods our veins here tonight. Some couples pair off seeking intimacy, and larger groups of people sidle off to plush seating areas, talking, teasing, touching one another while others look on.

Entranced by the change of atmosphere, I step out from my cover and weave my way through the throngs of people. The dancing is no longer prim and seemly, fit for high society. Looking around I see hands sliding along legs to expose thighs, tongues trailing across necklines, and hips pulsing together as the resonant sounds of a cello draw out a sensuous beat.

Spinning in place, I catch the eye of a woman leaning against a

nearby pillar, one arm lifted above her head as her hand grips the sloping black granite. Her mouth is subtly parted, lips pursed as she smiles
wickedly at me. Her other hand strokes along the soft skin of her décol-
letage, then with a flat palm she pushes it down her bosom and below
her belly. My eyes hungrily follow it, leading my vision to the sight of
her skirt pushed up around her waist, another woman kneeling before
her, head buried beneath the voluptuous folds of fabric.

Upper teeth curling over my bottom lip, I suck in a breath as the
woman's eyes flutter closed, an obscene moan curling from her throat
into the air.

Orgies spring up in every corner of the room, dancers grow lewder
and more unconcerned with public perception. A long-forgotten sensation tingles deep in my belly, and I swallow the thick, hot air.

Suddenly feeling parched, I move to the banquet tables, mouthwa-
tering with hunger and thirst. Fat, juicy grapes, slides of roast duck,
trays of figs and dates all look delicious, but the goblets full of fragrant
wine are calling to me, begging to be drunk.

Reaching for one of the glasses, I can feel the weight of someone's
eyes on the back of my neck.

Turning around, I meet the gaze of Helene, looking at me from her
seat high above the lascivious crowd. She inclines her head at me with a
challenging stare, lifting her wine in a toast.

Wishing only to honor her, I return the gesture, bringing the cup to
my lips.

16

Inhaling the saccharine aroma of the wine, I close my eyes as the liquid brushes against my lips. Parting them to welcome the drink, my tongue pushes forward, eager for a taste, when a hand wraps roughly around my wrist.

A woman turns me to her, gently taking the goblet from my hand and setting it back down on the table. A bubbly laugh rolls off her lips as she pulls me into the middle of the room, away from the tables of food and drink.

"Dance with me!" She giggles wildly, tossing her head back in an elaborate arc. Finding an empty spot amidst the throng of dancers, she clutches me closely to her, pressing her hips to mine. Staring up into my eyes, candlelight dances across her amber irises. She winds her arms around me, placing my hand on her waist. "Dance with me." This time, her words are a whisper, crossing the intimate distance between us on a breath that tickles my lips.

Shifting her hips, she begins to move, writhing against my body and I can feel myself whimper as I give in to the feel of her flesh pressed close to mine. We dance together, a slow, salacious back and forth as we spin together in the middle of the floor. I close my eyes, lips dipping to touch the outline of her ear, inhaling her sweet scent. My hand leaves its perch on her hip, roaming across her satin gown, fingertips softly pressing into her breasts as they rise above the sweeping low neckline.

Looping her arms around my neck, she pulls my face even with hers and whispers into my ear. "Are you in there, my scoundrel? Do you know who I am?"

On we dance, our movements growing more enticing with every step. The woman pulls back to look into my eyes and somehow through the lustful haze I see something more; an intense and searching gaze, both scared and caring, desperate to break through and reach my soul.

"It's me. It's your Meg."

All at once, every detail of her appearance falls into place like a puzzle being laid together. *Meg! She's alright!*

"It is you!" I pull her flush to me, breathing in her scent, sinking my fingers into her hair, memorizing the feel of her cheek pressed to mine. All these hours of searching and she is here, with me. Every injury, every fear, every doubt and terror I have endured is worth it, to see her here now. "Meg! Thank the goddess you're alright. I am so sorry I left you in the woods. I will never forgive myself for doubting you. I'm so sorry!"

Filled with overwhelming emotion, my footsteps falter, causing me to stumble, but she catches me and keeps upright. "We can discuss this later, but right now you must not fall! We need to keep dancing. Helene must believe that the curse still holds!"

Turning my hands in hers, she dances in a circle around me, eyes locked on mine. Meg is alive. Alive and in her present mind! Not bewitched, but simply Meg, the courageous and clever woman I fell for.

The woman I fell for.... The woman... I love.

If you had told me that tonight I'd be standing in an underground castle under the watchful eye of an evil sorceress, recently bewitched, and trapped with no simple way to escape, I'd have not believed you. Should you have added this here and now to be the moment I realize I've fallen in love? That would have been simply inconceivable.

And yet I have. I've fallen for her deeply. As much as I've fought it, for all that I've denied it, the overwhelming love I have for this woman is something I can no longer ignore. A shiver ripples through my skin, red-hot layers of painful heat seeming to melt from my flesh and suddenly I feel like I can breathe again. Clouds of black smoke drift across my vision, and my head clears fully, staring back into those eyes like pools of whisky. I want to tell her, to give her everything, but even I know that admitting to such a thing spells nothing but disaster for a thief and a princess. And so I whisper her name again like a prayer spoken into the wind.

"Meg..." My voice trails, every nerve in my body singing at her proximity. Twisting before me, she dances in sensual waves, stepping in and out of my embrace with the music's pulsing rhythm. She moves gently and easily and fits so well into my arms, and I trace my fingertips down her cheek. Suddenly realizing how we are holding each other and how her soft curves press into mine, my limbs stiffen in embarrassment, fumbling through my words. Flashes of how I held her, how I touched her while dancing just moments before... a swell of heat blossoms in my cheeks as shame floods through me. "Meg, I... I'm sorry. I wasn't myself, I-"

She slides a finger along my lips, keeping with the ruse of the dance far better than I am able to do. "It wasn't you. Not really. Though, I dare to say you do not mind it even now." Her eyes sparkle with a challenge, and I can feel my blush deepen.

"I would never act in a way to make you uncomfortable."

"I know." Her reply is honest and open and the implications that whirl through my head have no time to take root; she subtly points to the banquet tables lining the dance floor. "Anyway, it wasn't really you. The wine is enchanted. All who drink or even touch it are ensnared by my sister."

Wistfully, she looks around the room. "My other sisters and everyone here are unknowing accomplices. They are fully bewitched, eager to do her will. She tempts with pleasures, and only lives for power. All of these innocent people, caught in her web, with no idea she is trapping them here, waiting to lead them to slaughter. She's been stealing them from the villages! Snatching them in the middle of the night and bringing them here to serve her will. Many are of magic themselves, but they cannot use it. She forbids it, suppresses it, until the time is right and they only see her will. She wishes to use them to build up an army, to conquer all of the Empire. They are imprisoned, both in their minds and in this magical realm." Suddenly the missing person posters click in my mind, and I suck in a breath at the horror.

Twisting around me, she breathes into my skin. "My sisters and I are luckier... We at least return to the world... though in the morning, not one of us will remember this." She risks a glance over her shoulder to her sister's position and whispers in my ear. "Pull me closer."

Sliding a palm across her back, I push aside the awkward feelings, and dip to bring our hips together. Pitching my voice low so only she can hear, I ask her what she means.

"No one will remember? I don't understand. It was you who told me of all of this."

She frowns, a look of worry embedding itself in the wrinkles of her forehead. "Not clearly, though."

"No... you couldn't be sure if all of this was a dream." Staring around me, seeing how utterly real this all is, that hardly seems possible; but now that I have felt the effects of this magic firsthand, I believe it.

"What of tomorrow? Will all of this seem a disjointed memory or dream again?"

"I'm not sure." She spins in my arms, pressing her back to me, entwining our arms at her waist. "For reasons I cannot understand, the magic seems to... treat me differently. Everyone else here is utterly and thoroughly under the influence of Helene's magic. Most nights I retain some small amount of my wit, aware of what is going on around me though I am powerless to resist!" Her lips draw to a thin, hard line, and I can see her struggle to master her emotions, managing all of her anger and fear. "My sister, she uses us! With no way to fight back, we are simply pawns in her game." Her voice disappears and I press my face down next to hers. Jaw trembling, she tries to force a smile. "The things I have been party to, in service to her whims! I had thought to end my life rather than continue with all of this!"

"Ssshhh!" Brushing my lips against her cheeks, I tighten my arms around her. "Do not give any more of your thoughts to this. Instead, look how strong you are. Look how brave you are! I know how hard you fight. I am so, so sorry for leaving you, and yet, you fought back. You survived, and now here we are, because of you. You stopped me from drinking the wine, when I was so close to being lost forever to Helene's spell."

Cupping her cheeks in my hands, I gently stroke my thumbs across the soft skin of her face. "I made it this far to find you, but I cannot do this alone. I need you."

She nods, a small tear trickling down the side of her nose. "I'm so scared."

"I know. I am too."

"How do we end this?"

I shake my head, slowly turning us in our dancing closer to the edge of the crowd. "I don't know, but I promise that whatever we do, we will do it together."

Once we spin and turn to the outside of the room, I slip her hand into mine. Smiling at her, hoping to bolster whatever confidence she may have left, I squeeze her palm.

"Do you see that door, just beyond those pillars?"

"Yes."

"When I say run, run."

A few more strides, and we make a final push towards the exit. Dipping her backwards in my arms, I trace my lips along her jaw until I can whisper in her ear.

"Whatever you do, don't let go of my hand."

Standing tall, I turn my head, for one last look at the head table, caught in the crosshairs of Helen's scorching look.

Gripping her hand tightly in mine, I wait for just the right moment. A man and woman rush by, giggling madly with eyes full of lust as they make their way towards a nearby chaise. Ducking behind them, I lock eyes with Meg, and mouth the word. "Run!"

We dash beyond the pillars and out the door, racing down the hallway at a full sprint. Knowing nothing except a need to put as much distance between the room and our bodies, I race down hallways that seem unending, taking random turns at every opportunity, sure that somewhere behind us are pursuers. The first few turns bring us face to face with random servants or partygoers, but none seem so interested in our pair's dash through the castle. The further we run, the quieter it gets and soon every hall is empty, every room is still. An eerie silence descends upon us and a strange feeling hovers in the air.

Slowing our steps, I hold a finger to my lips. Meg nods, pressing a hand to her chest as she tries to quiet her labored breathing. We walk cautiously forward and the silence seems to grow, swallowing all sounds until I cannot hear even our own soft footfalls or the air rising and falling through our lungs.

We round a corner and a long hall stretches on before us with a lone door set into the far wall, a strange blue light seeping through the cracks.

Approaching it slowly, I try the door but it doesn't open. Meg tugs on my hand, and I turn to face her. Eyes wide and frightened, she shakes her head. Pulling the key from my pocket, I slip it into the lock, and turn. With no sound, I close my eyes, focusing on the feel of the lock in the door, turning slowly until I can feel the pins engage.

With a deep breath, I push open the door, blinking in the blue light that floods my sight. Once my eyes adjust, I can make out the figure of a woman, suspended in air, encircled in a vivid blue halo. I blink, tossing my head side to side, waiting for the details to become clear.

A soft brow, thin lips, and broad shoulders... all framed in the chestnut brown hair with a signature silver streak.

Before I can run to her, before I can reach for her, a scream rips through the still air, almost shaking me with the force of it. The woman's eyes fly open with alarm, opening her mouth as if to shout at me. She lifts her arm, pointing just behind me, a look of abject terror on her face.

I hear my mother's voice screaming inside my head, shouting my name. And just as I turn to look behind me, a blade is pressed against the side of my neck.

17

"Don't. Fucking. Move."

A voice as cold as steel hits my ears, and a shiver runs up my spine but I only have eyes for my mother. Her eyes are locked with mine, pleading desperately, though for what I don't know. My fingers flinch, tempted to reach for my blade, and she shakes her head with a miniscule motion. Relaxing my hand, I pull my eyes from her with monumental effort and try to make sense of everything around me.

From the corner of my eye, I can see a large man draped in a heavy woolen cloak, the hood pulled over his face. Shining silver buttons with small emeralds gleam along the front, but even if I hadn't seen those, I would recognize that voice anywhere.

He stands next to me, right arm outstretched with my mother's dagger clenched in his fist, point pressed against the side of my neck... but my fear surges when I notice that Meg is pressed to his front, a second knife laid across her throat.

I've fought a lot of opponents in my life, many of them larger and stronger. Never one to waste an opportunity, I've taken lessons from each of my confrontations and one thing I'm certain of is this: there is a fine line - but a vital one - between where anger bubbles over, leading to careless mistakes, and where anger takes over, ending things quickly. I am absolutely positive that Sam hates this new life. Once a man whose name was feared by so many, he is now long forgotten, forced to work in the squalor of a stable, his only path to restoring his name working as the grunt to a power-hungry sorceress. And that means I am certain he isn't allowed to kill me just yet. Leaning on that knowledge, I try to create an opening.

"Well, if it isn't Corvus, patron saint of bootlickers everywhere. Or... should I call you Sam?" Two slow, barely shifting steps and I turn just the slightest amount to face him more fully.

"Sam?" Meg's voice gasps out his name at the realization, a layer of hurt adding to her terror.

"You just can't keep your nose where it belongs, can you?" He sneers at me, upper lip curling over his teeth. "You're going to be so much fun to kill."

"Have at it then. You've clearly got me at a disadvantage, just end me already!"

I can see Meg begin to panic, the reality of the situation dawning in her head. She looks at me, shock very real in her eyes. "Please, Sam..." Tears begin to trickle down her cheeks as she begs him. "Please!"

"Shut up!" Sam hisses at her and based on Meg's whimper of pain, I'm sure the knife has dug just a little deeper into her skin.

The blade at my throat presses in as Sam leans closer to me. "Well I guess it's time for the happy reunion, then. Say hello to your sweet mum!"

He grins at me, teeth gleaming in the strange blue glow. "Althaea! It's a big day for you. You've got guests!" He looks once more at me, eyes traveling up and down my figure. "Knew who you were the second I laid eyes on you. You're the spitting image!"

The magnitude of everything in the past few hours overwhelms me, but I know if I don't keep my wits about me, I'll never survive. Corvus' smile shows that hint of excessive pride so well known to the criminally deranged, and I latch onto it, hoping for information.

"So you've known all along then. You're smarter than I gave you credit for, Sam. To think I worked for you so closely and never saw the brilliance hiding behind your rough exterior."

Manipulating him carefully, I layer insult with praise, hoping to trap him. "Of course, how could I, when you were nothing more than a fat old man who smelled worse than the horses? What was it, then? Twenty-two long years you were forced to live as the nobody you are, Helene stringing you along with promises of future glory?"

"Shut UP!" He roars at me, the blade at my throat shaking ever so slightly, and I can feel the prick of Avalonian metal drawing a drop of blood from my skin. "She'd be lost without me. I was the one who found you and figured out your mother must have found a way to summon you! I was the one who helped Helene with this binding spell!" He rips open the top of his shirt, a magical branding visible just over his heart. The burn is still fresh and looks deadly. Whether the infection is magical or natural I cannot tell, but the skin streaks in red tendrils reaching out in every direction. Unless it is treated, I can imagine sepsis will take hold. "She would never have succeeded without me!" Spittle flies in every direction as he screams at me, working so very hard to convince himself of his own words.

In an instant, the temperature of the room plunges, and I suddenly cannot move. Eyes darting around, I can see that Meg and Sam, too, are trapped in this stasis, warm breaths visible in the frigid air the only movement in the room. Helene stands in the doorway, the crow sitting on her shoulder, a look of disdain on her face.

She steps over the threshold and passes between us, pushing Sam's outstretched arm down and my mother's blade away from my neck with a look of disgust painted on her face. Her expression hardens once more as she strides across the room, making straight for my mother. I try to shout but have no voice, my screaming stuck inside my head.

Reaching through the blue misty light, she grasps my mother's jaw in her hand, squeezing it tightly.

"I hope it was worth it, Althaea. Your little spell may have worked, but now your daughter is going to die by my hand; and you're going to watch."

Releasing my mother, she turns to stare at our little ensemble, an almost bored expression on her face.

"This was supposed to be a wonderful night." She sighs dramatically. "Once every two hundred years, a blue moon aligns perfectly with the black star, and all magic is at its strongest. It is the black star that gave us magic ten thousand years ago when it shone into a quartz embedded into the slopes of the Obsidian Mountain. Tonight, the black star and blue moon align once more, and my plans are guaranteed." Turning to us once more, she dons a look of false pity. "I'm afraid your little rebellion is too late, but I do so hate that you disrupted my celebration."

She blinks, and the feeling of magical binding releases us, causing me to fall to the ground. Barely able to breathe, I clutch at my chest, gasping for air. Sam grabs Meg and pulls her to the side, holding her in an iron grip no matter how desperately she struggles. Helene paces towards me, a twisted look of fury on her face, one hand outstretched, fingers curled towards each other as if she is strangling me.

Instantly, my soul feels fragmented, breaking into a thousand miniscule pieces, drifting through the air towards her outstretched arm. Each breath more painful than the last, I force myself to inhale, but the oxygen doesn't come.

I can hear Meg just beyond my vision, sobbing in Sam's arms. Drifting my eyes past Helene, I gaze upon my mother's face. "I'm sorry..." I whisper. And my tears begin to fall.

Her eyes carry decades of grief and sorrow, and she looks at me with all the love I've been denied for so many years.

Meg shouts behind me, begging for her sister to stop. "Helene! Please! Let her go! I'll go with you; I'll do whatever you want but please let her go!"

My mother's eyes flit to the commotion, and then widen in shock, darting back to mine with desperation plain on her face.

"The dagger!" She mouths at me, eyes flicking towards Sam and Meg once more.

Every fire begins with the tiniest spark, and I can feel one roar within me, a rush of heat pushing back against the glacial influence of Helene's magic.

Seizing the momentary burst of adrenaline, I scream at Meg. "The meadow! Remember the meadow!"

Meg's eyes fly to mine, and flash with fury and fear. Hands flying to her throat, I can see her suck in a breath as she spins towards the blade, wincing as the tip of the knife slices a thin line through her skin. Sam jolts in surprise at her movement, and Meg jams her foot down as hard as she can, seizing the moment to spin from Sam's arms as the knife clatters to the floor. The distraction is all I need. Helene's magic wavers for a split second, and I push from the ground and sprint towards them. Charging at Sam, I barrel between his body and Meg's as I duck under his left arm, pushing it to the side. I spin behind him, wrapping my fingers around his right hand and forcefully turn the knife into his middle, my mother's blade sinking deep into his belly. I twist and pull, crying in pain as I free it from his flesh. My ears fill once more with an overwhelming humming sound, and the blade vibrates, growing warm in my hand. The Avalonian metal begins to glow, and as the last of my strength fades, I summon my final effort and heave the dagger through the air towards my mother.

It pierces through the blue orb of light and she catches it cleanly, the magic around her shattering into a million pieces as she falls to the floor.

Collapsing, I fight to stay awake. Meg rushes to my side and pulls me to the corner of the room. I writhe in pain, the sound of Helene's screaming echoing in my ears, but I cannot look away. My mother rises to her full height, and I watch as the stones on my mother's dagger begin to shine, light increasing to a blinding outburst that fills the room like an explosion. When the light clears, she is standing before Helene, the two squaring off with one another.

"This ends now, Helene!" My mother shouts at her, dagger gripped securely at her side.

A frightening laugh burns low in Helene's throat, slowly gaining volume and speed, ending in a shriek of laughter as she tosses back her head. "You think this is over? You are a fool if you think you can end this! The greatest healer of all time you may be, but you are no match for my power. You could not even save her mother with your tricks!" Pointing at Meg, Helene grins a sinister smile. "I was only a girl and able to change the course of history, ending the queen and imprisoning you. You have nothing to use against me! Nothing! Only in fairytales do heroes win. In truth, dark always triumphs over light, and I will be the one to restore Gormliath to its glory, no matter what I must do!"

My mother raises her arm above her, a vivid gold light gathering in her palm. "You should have known, Helene, but your pride has been your greatest weakness all along. You have never seen the truth! It was no mistake that the queen died, nor that you captured me. You've never been able to wrap Meg up in your evil because she is protected; protected by a spell her mother ordered me to cast! She gave her own life out of love for her child and her kingdom, and I have been waiting over twenty long years to defeat you. So yes, Helene. This ends now."

Pulling her arm back, she thrusts it forward, golden light shooting from her palm. With a snarl, a pillar of black smoke swirls up around Helene, blasting the light in every direction. It rattles the room and the floor rumbles with the force of a mountain crumbling. Cracks splinter up the walls, and when the smoke finally disappears, Helene is gone.

My mother runs to me, kneeling beside me. With a last look at the gurgling heap that is Corvus, she presses her hands to my chest.

"What happened? Is she dead?" I wearily ask.

"No, my darling. She is not dead." Closing her eyes, her lips begin to move, a crushing weight pushing down against my sternum the only sensation I can feel. Her eyes open under heavy lids, a look of anguish on her face. Trying once more, she pushes more firmly, lips flying through an incantation.

"What are you doing?" Meg asks fearfully, nervous and bewildered.

"I cannot heal her. My magic. It is gone."

She rests a beat, then quickly moves to her feet. "You must help me. We have to leave. We cannot stay here."

With much concentration and effort, the two of them lift me to my feet, and we rush from the room, my lungs protesting with every step. I feel sluggish and weighty, barely able to lift my feet even with their support.

Down the stairs we move, stumbles and near falls threatening our escape. But when we reach the landing at the bottom, a rumble shakes the castle with all the impact of a landslide.

Dust falls from the ceiling, a new quake following, another shortly after.

"The castle is collapsing!" Meg cries out just as a piece of the ceiling breaks free and falls just before us, nearly crushing her.

"We must move!" Their grips tighten, fingers digging into my sides and we move, rushing down a nearby hall. "This way!" Meg shouts, guiding us. They race as fast as they can, narrow misses and closed off corridors blocking our escape until we round a corner and there is nowhere left to go. Meg's eyes dart back and forth, searching her brain for a solution, and she steers us back until we reach one of the doors set in a long hallway. Flinging it open, we rush inside. "This is the only way out." We stand before a window, the sloping ground some ten feet below us. "Do you... Do you think you can you make it?" She stares at me, fear flooding her eyes.

Feigning strength I do not have, I can see it all laid clearly before me. Knowing that my mother and Meg will never go without me, and certain I do not have the strength to safely hang from the window until the drop is smaller, I lean into the windowsill and pull my legs to the other side. "Come and get me!" With a smile, I push from the window, flying towards the ground.

18

The impact never comes. Or at least, there is no bone-shattering pain in my legs as they slam into the ground. Instead I feel only softness as my feet gently hit the grass outside the window. What on earth?! Confused and alarmed, I look up and see my mother grin and Meg gape at me from the window. The earth trembles once more, and I lose my balance. With no time for questions, I shout up at them.

"Meg! Jump!" She scrambles into the window frame and slides out, hanging by her fingertips. "I've got you," I call to her. She sucks in a breath and lets go.

Falling into my arms, I grasp her tightly, inhaling her scent, whispering adorations into her hair.

"You can stand! You're alright!" Her voice is bewildered but joyful, and she tightens her arms around me.

Quickly kissing her forehead, I set her aside and look up at my mother. Without waiting for assistance, she pushes through the window and drops steadily to her feet. Walking towards Meg and I, her eyes shine with happiness, staring at me with wonder. "My darling..." She reaches us, then pulls us into her arms.

A sudden crack of lightning flashes across the sky, the sound so loud it feels as if my head is split in two. Looking up, a current of purple and white light stretches out in every direction from the stone set into the tallest tower of the castle. "The crystal!" My mother shouts. Another flash of lightning and the crystal's light begins to pulse, brightening with every flicker.

"It's unstable! We have to leave, now!"

She races off towards the lake and we follow, stumbling with every tremble of the earth beneath our feet. Cracks erupt from the ground at our feet, shooting up the hillside in a fraction of a second. Moving so fast I feel as if my feet barely touch the ground, the boats soon come into view. Just as we reach them, the castle makes a groaning noise, upper floors crumbling in upon themselves.

Meg stops and turns, screaming at the castle. "My sisters!"

"There's no time!" I grab her hand, pulling her towards the boats. "Meg! There's no time! This entire place is going to fall. We have to get back to Gormliath!"

Hating myself for it, I pull her into a boat with my mother, fighting against Meg's kicks and screams. Wrenching an arm free from my grasp, she reaches desperately through her sobs for the people still visible, dancing away inside and completely oblivious to the end of the world around them.

Grabbing an oar, my mother pushes us from the shore, rowing with all her strength, refusing to look back. I cradle my love in my arms, holding her tight as the sobs rack her body, mourning the loss of her sisters and the grief of what is to come.

The lake grows rough as the journey continues and my mother's jaw tightens, muscles straining with the effort. Waves rock us violently from side to side, and I move a hand from Meg's shoulders to grip the edge of the boat. At last, we reach the shore as the waves threaten to engulf us. We scramble from the boat and up the shore, and I turn just in time to see the waves pull the boat back out into their tumultuous depths.

Above us on the hill, the light glitters and shines under the surreal starlight. Seeing the diamond forest stretch out before me, my body wants to rebel. The thought of braving the cursed woods that stand between us and safety makes my knees weak. But just as I gather my inner strength, determined to go on, a flash of red catches my eye and I snap my head up, chasing it. Helene stands at the top of the hill, looking down at us, her eyes staring deeply into mine. I lunge for her, but she disappears from sight, and the trees rise from the earth, roots pushing them upwards until they crash to the ground, blocking the path. Tree after tree goes down, sealing off our exit as Helene races for the safety of her earthly kingdom. We are trapped.

"Meg?" I look to her, trying to hide the desperation in my voice, tilting her still quivering chin up so I can see her face. "Is there any other way home?"

She shakes her head gently and I can feel dread curling up in my belly, this never-ending nightmare seeming to have finally met its end.

"Yes there is." My mother's voice is quiet, but strong. Walking past us, she steps to the edge of the glittering trees, then turns and faces the darkness.

We follow her, stopping just at the point where the impenetrable darkness seems to begin. Without a word, she hands me her dagger.

The moment my fingers close around the handle, a burst of light flows from the blade, piercing the darkness before us. In awe, I raise my hand, observing the dagger from every angle. A warmth spreads up my arm and through me, erasing every ache, pain, and injury. "Mother?"

Guiding my hand, she walks me forward, Meg holding tightly to my other arm. Into the darkness we walk, until there is nothing around us but black.

Meg's grip tightens on my arm, and I hug her to my side, trying to appear less frightened than I feel.

As we go deeper and deeper into the abyss, the sounds from the collapsing castle are slowly left behind, and the ground stills under our feet. There is nothing. Nothing but the three of us, moving onward in no direction at all through the darkness, guided only by the beam of light that streams from the tip of the dagger.

"What is this place?" Meg's voice is small, but curious. Mother almost laughs in her reply, a sound that feels both out of place and welcome, considering our present circumstances.

"We are between two worlds, little dove. But we are going home."

The journey seems to drag on forever and with each step I find myself growing restless and more anxious, sure that we are to be stuck forever in this unending black. My mother reaches out a hand and lays it on my shoulder, and we continue to walk on.

After what feels like hours, the sword's light dims, the beam of light reaching a finite point in the distance. Picking up the pace, we move towards it, eager for something - anything - that feels like ground beneath my feet and air above my head. At last, there is the sound of rushing water, growing louder and louder with each approaching step, and then the light goes out.

Instantly, a curtain of water flowing at crushing speeds is before us, the dull light of dawn just beyond.

I reach my hand out but the water is too strong, and I fear that crossing under the force of it may prove impossible. Helpless once more, I can feel the bulk of the dagger in my hand, and the gentle thrumming in my palm. Lifting it before me, I extend it and push it into the cascading streams, praying that it doesn't fly from my hand with the weight of the water's fall.

Instead, the water parts, rising like a curtain away from the blade, and I thrust it further in, watching in awe as the water ceases to fall altogether.

Wearing a smile of pride and relief, my mother walks past me and pushes through the veil, wading into a now-still river just beyond.

I leap forward, whooping in delight as the real world takes shape before my eyes, the feel of water on my legs so solid and familiar. I hold my hand out to Meg who steps through behind me, a complicated look on her face. Tilting my head up to the sky, I close my eyes and feel the warmth of the sun's rays, and I cannot help but laugh.

The three of us wade to the river's edge and settle onto the shore, drying off in the sun. Meg grabs at her sodden skirts and I hand her the dagger, which she takes, slicing the fabric over and over until she can break free from the many layers. She gives it back to me without a word, staring off into the distance.

"Meg..."

My mother clears her throat. "Leave the girl be. She needs more time."

We sit on the river's bank, bedraggled and exhausted, more questions than answers swirling in my brain. Coming to sit between the two of us, my mother picks up the dagger once more, placing it in my hands.

I look at her, finding a proud smile on her face.

"It is you, my darling."

"What do you mean? Mother, what does all of this mean?"

Her eyes are gentle and full of love, and she places her hand on the side of my face. "My mother was a great healer, bestowed with the gift of magic by her mother, who was given it by her mother, and so on, and so forth. We have no ordinary magic, though. Our magic only works to heal, never to hurt, and our connection to Alea, the goddess of healing, is channeled through these stones." Her fingers reach out, tracing the trifecta of gemstones set into the hilt of the weapon. "We are the only healers with magic that I know of, able to erase curses and cure all disease, even beyond typical small injuries and illness. Our magic, however, is a closely guarded secret, and we must be selective in when and how we use it. If we so much as attempt to end a life... the magic leaves us. It is a sacred duty."

She sighs, staring off into the distance across the river which flows once more. "I was so certain that you would be the one to carry on this mission, but I left you before you reached your time of womanhood, when the magic blooms inside." She strokes my face gently, and I can see the decades of sadness written on her face. "Oh, my daughter, how I wish I could have stayed. I hated myself for leaving you then."

"Then why did you?" The words come out angrier than I realize, years of hurt rising to the surface.

"Because of her." She looks to Meg, a strange expression on her face. "The Queen summoned me, and her correspondence was desperate. After marrying the king, she was soon with child. The eldest daughter, a young woman in her own right by that point, had a heart full of hate, so distraught by the circumstances around her mother's end. As she saw how the king doted on his new queen and praised her so openly,

her animosity grew, and dark magic awoke within her. Working in secret lest she be killed herself, she targeted the queen. Everything from
poisoned herbs tucked beneath her pillows to falling down stairs, the
queen's spies learned that Helene was determined to end her life; and
the life of her unborn child.

"She wrote to me of the great evil that was to come. She knew that
Helene was smart but proud, and that resentment is a powerful affliction. Knowing that my magic cannot be used to kill, lest it leave me forever, she asked instead for help."
Meg looks at us now, listening. My mother turns, telling the rest of the
story directly to her.

"When I arrived, the queen was very nearly ready to deliver. Disguised as a midwife, I waited with her for two weeks until the time
came, and you came into this world, pink and beautiful with a cry as
loud as an eagle's scream." My mother gently touches Meg's chin, a sad
smile on her face. "There is a protective spell that makes one resistant
to magic. Nothing can remove the effects all together, but with this rit-
ual, one can be saved from its most dangerous influence. Your mother
begged me to do it, certain that one day, Helene would rise to power
through magical means, and you would be the only one who could stop
her."

"Me?" Meg's voice is as quiet as a whisper, hanging in the still air
around us.

"Yes, you. If you could not be taken under her spell, you could find a
way to end this, and restore the kingdom. Your mother believed in you
from the moment you were born."

Meg stares at her, and I can see disbelief in her eyes. "That's impossible! I am powerless against Helene. Think of how easily I was taken, ab-
ducted in the forest by Sam, and how quickly I fell back under her spell!
I could hear myself, see myself, even feel the way I went along with her!"

"Did you ever truly, though? Were you completely and utterly mind-
less? Or did you find some part of you still able to cling to reason,
knowing that what went on around you was not just a dream, but real
life?"

Meg sits in stunned silence, and my mother takes her hands in her own. "Do not fear the future. Your mother's love protects you. She gave her very life so that I could cast the spell, and I held you closely to me until the soldiers pried you from my arms."

I cannot help the exclamation that bursts past my lips. "I knew you would never kill anyone!"

A burst of laughter flies from my mother's mouth, but a very sad smile takes over. "I tried to. Just then, in the castle. But Helene got away before the spell could complete."

Piecing together the information, I am stunned. "If you could have killed her all along, why not do it earlier?"

"It would never have worked." She says it simply, as if explaining an obvious point. "Helene is the most powerful sorceress to have ever lived. After my capture, she had me moved to a prison deep in the Midnight Kingdom, telling her father I had disappeared, thus feeding his descent into fear and madness. She used magic to bind me within a room, isolated except for times when she and Corvus came together. But I am no longer a young woman, and if I had tried, Corvus would have killed me before the magic had completed its course. No, I had to be more careful. And even if I had succeeded, and somehow survived, my magic would have been lost forever for killing her. And so I spent years growing my magic in secret, keeping it strong and ready, until the time was right. I summoned you to Gormliath, in the hopes that we would meet and I would pass the magic on to you."

She exhales a breath, almost a laugh, and looks at me with fondness. "You always did have a way of landing right into the thick of things. When Sam came down and told me he saw a woman who was my mirror image, well, it didn't take them long to figure it out. In a rage, Helene trapped me, frozen in time forever. I don't know how long you've been here since, but only your voice woke me from her enchantment, and only you could have broken it with my knife, that I now give to you."

She gently wraps my fingers around the handle, pressing it into my lap. "I know I have placed an immeasurable burden upon you both, but

Helene's final act is here. With the power of the crystal, her magic will be at its height, and the kingdom is poised to fall to her." She rests one hand on my shoulder, and the other on Meg, speaking to us each in turn. "It is only with your gifts, and Meg's resistance to magic, that the outcome can change. It is the two of you who are the only ones to break the spell."

19

"But how?"

"I'm afraid I cannot tell you." She strokes my hair, gazing tenderly into my eyes. "You possess the magic now. It became yours the minute I tried to end Helene's life. You only needed to take it for your own."

"And that happened when I jumped out of the window?"

"It appears so."

She stands, brushing off her skirts, wringing as much of the dampness as she can from the cloth. "Look. The sun has risen. It is a new day."

Following her gaze, I see the orb glowing just above the horizon, ushering in a new dawn. Who knows what will happen, between now and its next ascent into the sky, but I realize now that I cannot wait. Too long I've been a passenger in life; now, I must take the reins.

I spring from my seat on the ground, dusting off my palms. Bending down, I offer my hand to Meg and she takes it, standing to rise with me.

"This is really happening, isn't it?"

"It is. Are you alright?"

Her answer is slow to come, contemplating my words, but when she responds, her voice doesn't waver. "I am." She squeezes my hand and I squeeze hers back and we stand there, looking into each other's eyes. Wondering if this is the beginning of the end of our story, I drink in every detail of her here before me.

A subtle cough behind me, I jolt and tear my eyes away from her.

"Sorry to end the moment, but it would do us all some good to eat before we return to the castle. And Meg, you'll need new clothes."

She blushes slightly at my mother's words, but nods, her stomach growling in consent. Looking around, the geography suddenly registers in my brain.

"I know where we are!"

Taking off at a sprint, I fly down the bank of the river, running full on into the woods. I can hear them shouting behind me as they try to follow.

Where is it, where is it, where is it?! Wracking my brain, I try to remember if it was really this far before. Just when the first doubt takes root in my mind, the building appears before me.

Running back to make sure the others see me, I call them over. "What is this place?" my mother asks.

"This was Corvus' home. And it should have everything we need."

Meg gasps, my mother grins, and I push open the door.

It is much as I remember it, though entering from this angle is a little disorienting and I look around to readjust my memories. Grabbing some fruit from the rack, I hand each of them one and bite into my own delicious pear.

The sweet, fragrant juices run down my chin and I wipe a hand across my face, licking every last drop that I can. Meg looks somewhat scandalized at my manners, but biting into her own, she does the same, closing her eyes to savor the taste. Giggling at her imitation, I bend and begin to light a fire, hoping that the warmth will cut some of the chill our wet clothes bring.

My mother turns and begins to rummage through the various baskets and jars, amassing a pile on the bed. Garlic, lavender, oils of different colors and consistencies, she pulls items from all over with a critical eye. I watch her for a few minutes, stoking the flames until a small, comforting blaze is crackling in the fireplace. "What are you looking for?"

"Anything and everything, my dear. I may no longer possess magic, but I am still a healer."

Finally, she kneels on the ground and opens the chest.

Pulling the blanket and top contents aside, she gasps when the tattered old cover of the grimoire comes into view.

Her eyes glare at the book, a look I cannot read on her face. She sits there staring for minutes that stretch on, until finally I inch a little bit closer.

"Mother?"

She jumps, drawn from her thoughts by my voice, and grabs for the book. Spinning on her knees, she throws the book directly into the fire.

Nothing should be able to shock me by now, but I am unprepared me for this. The book begins to scream, a shriek so profound that all three of us cover our ears and shrink to the ground, desperate for the noise to end. Flames lick the edges of the binding but the book does not burn. Watching in desperation, I shove my hands into the fire and pull the book out, beating it with the sheets from the bed. The screaming dies down as the flames extinguish, and we stare at the grimoire in terror.

"What... was that?"

My mother's eyes are fixated on the book, a look of horror and disgust on her face. "It is worse than I feared. Helene's magic is almost limitless, and that book is bound to her soul. It cannot be destroyed so long as she is alive. But trust one thing, she knows that we have it."

"Is she coming? Does she know where it was hidden?"

The words have barely left Meg's lips when the fire flickers and goes out, an unnatural darkness descending on the glen.

Meg jumps up behind me, clutching my shoulders and peeking out of the window with a whimper. "This... this isn't right."

"No, it's not." My mother's voice is almost a snarl and she stands before us, arms slowly stretching out in protection. "She's here."

A thick black tunnel of smoke forms from the gathering clouds and descends to earth, swirling violently into bright red streaks. The red melts and streaks into ribbons, gathering in formation until the full form of Helene's dress comes into view, her very body seeming to materialize from the smoke, black veins creeping across her porcelain skin.

"Oh, goddess protect us!" Meg's terrified voice bursts in a whisper over my shoulder, her fingernails digging into my back.

"Well, well, well." Helene stalks toward, eyes wild and full of insanity. In her hand, she clutches a heavy dagger with a black handle, and I can just make out the sheen of blood running down the edge of her blade, dripping into the soft grasses.

"It was ever so kind of you to call me, Althaea! Rather stupid, though, powerless as you are! I should have dispatched you years ago, with how utterly pitiful your magic is!"

My mother steps forward, pushing through the door before I can stop her. I lunge for her, trying in vain to grasp at her sleeve as she steps outside, fully exposed to the lethal magic before her.

"Then why didn't you? You really believed Corvus? That you could use my magic? I thought you were nobody's fool, but he really strung you along, didn't he?"

Meg's fingers drum an urgent tattoo against my back, anxiety tapping her fingers in a stuttered rhythm. Her whisper is hoarse and frantic. "What is she doing? Helene will kill her! Why is she taunting her?"

I lift a solitary finger to my lips, flicking my eyes to her. "Just... trust her," I mouth to Meg.

"You could never possess my magic, little girl. My magic belongs only to those who believe in good. My magic is innate, born into me from birth. When used to help, to heal - my power is limitless! Hate grew your magic, and your power is bound by the shackles of your heart! You will never be the great sorceress you wish to be, Helene. You are destined to be nothing but a distant memory, forgotten by this generation and those to come."

Helene's face distorts, looking almost inhuman. The black spidery veins that push against her skin seem to pulse with every beat of her heart, and she howls her words at my mother. "How dare you! You speak of destiny? I will be remembered through all of time as the greatest queen to have ever lived. And who are you? You speak of your magic as if you still possess it, as if it still lives! But I watched you lose it - I felt you lose it! It is dead, and so you shall be too!"

An orb of black feathers gathers in her hand, whipping around in a frenzy. Lifting her hand above her head, the feathers seem to take the shape of an arrow, and my heart plummets to the ground.

"You're wrong!" I'm out the door before I know it, instinct pushing me forward.

Helene's head snaps in my direction, the feathers falling to her feet. "You!" Barely a heartbeat later, the feathers gather together again and are hurtling through the air on a direct course for my chest.

Okay, magic... Now would be a great time to kick in.

I throw my hands up in front of me, palms out, desperately hoping for... anything. Squinting one eye open, I barely have time to see the dozens of little black arrows fly straight into my body.

"No!" I can hear Meg screaming in the distance, the bizarre form of her shredded gown flying towards me across the sloping ground.

So this is what death feels like. Warm, sticky, and so, so disorienting. I crumple to the floor, staring down at my chest in disbelief. My head tips back and I stare up at the distant canopy, vision blurring in and out. My mother's face pushes into my sight, hands shaking. "Darling, give me your hands!" She gathers my limp appendages in hers, pressing them against the wounds peppering my skin. The magical weapons are gone, with only their sickly dark holes left as evidence of their presence.

"Well, that was easy, wasn't it?" Helene's voice is mocking, a demented cackle cutting into her words. "Who's next?" She paces in the grass nearby, her fingers dancing in a teasing children's game as she chooses her next target.

Meg and my mother pay her little mind. My eyes flit between them, looking at the two women I love with all of my soul. Meg sits beside me, her eyes wide with fear and desperation. My mother's face stands in stark contrast, her brows knit together with determination and urgency.

"Listen to me!" She whispers loudly, the hiss flinging droplets of moisture onto my face. "You must feel it! You must feel the life force within you! Find it and latch on to it. You can heal yourself!"

What a silly woman. She must be mad, thinking this isn't how I meet my end. I chuckle at her naivety, the smile on my face disappearing as my laughter dissolves into choking on the blood that fills my throat.

Coughing violently, I roll onto one side, eyes sliding closed. Through fuzzy hearing, I can just make out Meg's sobs, my mother's insistent directions, and Helene's disturbed enjoyment of this scene.

What a shitty way to die. I never got to learn this magic. I never got to tell my mother I forgive her for leaving all those years ago. And I never got to kiss the woman I love.

Oh. Wait. The softest feeling presses into my blood-stained lips, something slipping away by the second, but something I can understand. She's kissing me. Now, I suppose I can die happy.

The feeling in my lips comes to an end, and I know that this is it. My heart shudders to a stop, and everything is silent.

20

I should be dead. I think I am dead. Aren't I? Isn't this how people die? My mind turns over and over, sorting through the possibilities of how I might not be dead yet, and finally I realize one thing. There's a cool breeze, a draft of sorts, escaping through the tips of my fingers. It tingles across my chest, through my toes, above my head. It's chilly and arid, and with a decent bit of force it flows away.

Stop that, I say to the breeze. *Don't leave me. It's not yet time.*

The air ceases its movement, hovering still.

Come back home.

There is a small shudder, and then the air flows backwards, racing back into every cavern caused by Helene's magic, until I feel like I've sucked in a burst of cold air.

That's better. Time to close the door.

And then, as if a match the size of a pinhead is struck, the tiniest flame builds warm and low in my belly. It stretches out, the hint of heat building through my torso, concealing the breeze and tucking it far away, safely down within. A dull warm glow seems to flow through my limbs, tingling in the tips of my fingers, and I press my fingers against my tattered skin.

Sweet, soft fire, like the dull warmth from dying embers dances all around me, sealing my breeze inside. I feel warmth and beauty and suddenly the air around me is singing, sweet voices drifting through the air like a summertime lullaby.

The song ends and my lungs burst alive, opening in a great heaving breath. My eyes fly open and I shoot up, sitting between my mother and Meg.

"You're alive!" The two of them shout in unison, Meg's more a question and my mother's an exclamation of surety. I smile at them, bizarrely both astounded at what just happened, and feeling as if an unfinished piece of a puzzle has finally been settled into its place.

A scream of outrage cuts through the air, so other-worldly it feels as if it rips into reality itself. Bursting to my feet, I glare at Helene, whose shoulders and breasts heave with every seething breath.

"Then I guess I'll kill you first!" She snarls and lunges for my mother, knife raised high in the air, her other hand opening to reveal flames licking against her skin. Before I can react, the flames shoot at my mother, engulfing her in a flash, and her screams tear at my very soul.

As if by nature, one of my hands flies out from my side, magic searing from my skin, streaming across the distance and dousing the flames. My mother collapses, her body tumbling to the ground, scorched and covered in patches of almost glowing red skin.

A flurry of movement from the corner of my eye is followed by a scream of fear. I turn to see Meg, enshrouded in a cloud of birds as they peck and scratch at her, a never-ending onslaught of attacks. At first her arms flail wildly, trying to keep them at bay, but soon she shrinks in upon herself, crouching with her arms wrapped over her neck and head, her sobs barely concealing her cries of, "Please! Stop! Helene, please!"

The anguish in her voice is utterly heartbreaking. Forcing down my own anger and pain, I hone in on the sound of rushing wings as they pursue my sweet Meg relentlessly. Pushing my magic to her, I focus all of my energy on her, trying to work past my hatred for Helene and focusing instead on my love for Meg. A sound like a gong ripples through the air, and a blast of magic reverberates all around me, slicing through the crowd of birds and disintegrating them all into nothing.

"You're nothing, and nobody, and I won't let you win!" Helene's attacks are ruthless, one after another, over and over again. It drags on for what feels like hours. My mother, Meg. My mother, and Meg; each time

I find myself more in tune to my magic and each time I grow more exhausted by its usage.

I look to the two of them, each one some twenty meters apart. I can see the brunt of damage that Helene's magic has taken. My mind rattles off the list of curses I've somehow pushed away, and I shudder at the thought of how much we have endured. Ice, flames, birds, spiders, blindness and hallucinations, even unseeable pain from the inside out; no part of the two of them untouched by Helene's evil. A dozen or more assaults on them, with me growing weaker by the minute. She targets me by targeting those important to me, wearing me down until I am unable to protect them, forced to watch them succumb.

Standing in the space between them, my heart wishes I could close the distance between them and feel their solid presence close to me. But that feels impossible. They are beaten down, bedraggled, weak, and burned. I have only enough in me to sustain my new and unfamiliar magic, but I know I must get help. My heart yearns to be near to Meg... but I know I must go to my mother. I need her help. I do not know how much longer I can do this.

Straining under the weight of my own wearied limbs, I take one final look at Meg's broken form, dazed and disoriented from the onslaught of injury. Whispering into the space between us, desperately hoping it somehow finds its way to her heart, I close my eyes and speak the words out loud. "I love you."

Then I turn and with monumental effort, lift my foot and take one single step towards my mother.

Helene's form flies from her standing point, materializing before me in a flash, a wicked grin on her face. "Nope."

She whirls around and hurtles her knife straight into my mother's chest, and in the same second she clenches her other hand into a tight fist, and I can feel my body's oxygen depleting.

"It was so much fun playing with you, little mouse," she sneers at my face as it purples beneath her magical grip, "but it is time to end this. Of course, you can heal yourself, but by the time you're back, your mother will be dead."

Her words seem distant, and the world falls away. All I can see is my mother, knees in the dirt, eyes wide and distraught as she clutches the knife embedded deep within her. Slowly, those gorgeous eyes, framed by that beautiful silver streak of hair, turn towards me. She stares at me unblinking for a minute, and then she smiles, folding in on herself and slumping into the earth.

"NO!" I scream silently. I claw at my throat, tears streaming down my face as I try to pry the magical fingers from my neck, but Helene's laughter pitches loudly across the clearing, pushing aside any other sound from my ears.

The utter despair I feel fills me, and the last thought I have before slipping into the waves of unconsciousness is how much I'd love to rip the still-beating heart from Helene's body the moment I am awake.

But then I hear a gasp, and the pressure on my throat disappears. I cough and vomit, every breath a searing pain that threatens to blind me. Forcing myself to see, I open my eyes and my stomach erupts once again, every new fear being realized in succession.

Meg hovers in the air behind Helene, poised mid-leap with my mother's dagger raised high. The point of the blade is within a hair's breadth of the back of Helene's exposed neck. Frozen in midair, unable to move, the wind swirls around us, whipping her hair across her face. Meg's face is pinched, the full extent of her pain visible as she fights to take action against all odds. But Helene somehow saw her coming, shifting her magic to cease all of Meg's movement, grasping Meg in her clutches.

"Well, if it isn't the beloved pure-hearted child, sinking so low as to try and murder her own doting sister in cold blood?" She circles her, left hand spread flat in midair as she controls her magic, the other stretching towards my mother's unmoving form. "Oh, what the people of Gormliath will think! That you, little one, could be so cruel! Why, it was you after all, that lead to the deaths of our sweet, innocent sisters, trapping them there forever, leaving them to die! And all because you thought yourself a better leader than me, unwilling to restore Gormliath to its former glory! We will mourn the others for ten weeks, each dedicated to one of their lovely lost souls. But on the eleventh week we will celebrate with dancers and feasts as we revel in your end! And this is the history that will stand the test of time, with my victory bringing safety from your evils and prosperity to my people!"

My mother's body convulses, and the knife rips free, soaring back into Helene's hand.

Meg suddenly snaps to a convex form, her fingertips almost brushing against the back of her legs, so tightly wound her body is now. She raises higher in the air, and with a snap of her fingers, a sickening crack splits through my ears and Meg's body sinks in upon itself, falling to the ground with an earth-shattering sound.

"Oh, little sister. Look what you made me do." Her tone drips with innocence and my anger reaches a boiling point as a bitter taste floods my mouth. Feeling a surge of inhuman strength, I lunge at her.

All I want to do is kill her. An overwhelming hatred surrounds me, filling my head with rage. I cannot think; I cannot reason. My instincts guide me, and I let them carry my movements as I close the space between us.

Just before my hands reach her skin, the broken form of my mother flashes by the corner of my vision, and her voice rings out in my head; a flood of information rushing through my brain. If we kill, our magic is lost forever. We are called only to heal. Helene's dark power was born of hatred. *What if I become like her?*

At the very last second, I twist out of the way. Everything is clear.

Landing hard on the ground, I roll a few meters and spring up onto my feet, one hand on the ground. I focus on the feel of the earth between my fingertips, the way the lush grasses and moss connect me to the oldest magic of all; life.

I take a deep breath, and every miniscule vibration of the planet ripples up through my fingers and fills my whole body. Every plant and flower around me seem to push breaths of cool, clean air directly into the deepest recesses of my lungs. The sun's rays warm my back, radiating a comforting presence all around me. I close my eyes, rise to my full height, and take determined, calm steps towards Helene.

The most bizarre feeling I've ever encountered bursts from my fingers, a power that seems to both drain my heart and strengthen it at once. My body feels lighter than air, yet each step lands solidly in the soft earth, all of my senses strengthened. My eyes fly open and a burst of gold, sparkling in the early morning sun, erupts from every inch of my body, enveloping me in a warm aura. Every ache, every pain melts away, and I feel a well of power bubble up from within, overpowering me and yet feeling so safe and so right.

Focusing on this feeling, I close my eyes once more, gathering it within me. It rolls and ebbs, the energy and power sucking into my core as the pressure slowly builds. I can hear Helene screaming at me from somewhere beyond my protective barrier, but a full and all-encompassing sense of peace is building within me, shutting out every negative, hurtful emotion and erasing all hate from my mind.

Healing. Love. Goodness. I want the world to be good again. I want to heal the world. *This is what I must do.*

The last of my power rushes into me, and then it bursts, exploding out into the world in a blinding light that shakes the trees and disrupts the waterfall.

When the light fades, and I can see again, I look around me. There is chaos everywhere, a large crater sunk into the ground, the four of us within it.

Helene is on the ground, slow breaths the only confirmation that she still lives. She shakily rises to her feet and stares at me, a complicated expression on her face. Anger, bewilderment, frustration, and desperation combine in her features, and yet... She looks... softer, somehow. The black veins are gone, and only the subtle rosy glow of exertion lights upon her cheeks.

She thrusts out a hand at me, grunting with effort. Nothing happens. Again she tries, angrily screwing up her face as she attempts over and over again to inflict magic upon my standing form.

"What have you done to me?" she shrieks. "What have you done?!"

"I healed you." The words come out simply, full in their explanation.

"Your magic was born of anger and hatred. It was a sickness of your heart. I healed you."

She sinks down into the dirt, a look of shock on her face, and she finally takes a minute to look around her. Slowly, she takes in the setting, the destruction, the damage, and the still fallen forms of her sister and my mother.

"This... was me?" Her eyes fall to her lap and I can see her lips begin to tremble as the fullness of the situation begins to dawn on her.

Bending down, I crouch before her, speaking softly. "And it is over now. Your magic is gone."

She looks up at me and begins to cry. Sobs wrack her body, and she pounds her fists in the dirt. "I'm sorry!" she wails. "I'm so sorry! What have I done?"

I drop to one knee in the dirt before her and rest a hand on her shoulder. There will be time for repentance, and time for her to be held accountable for her crimes. But for now... I rub her shoulder soothingly, waiting for her cries to cease.

The tears do stop, quieting to a low rumble and I push off from the dirt, ready to move along. Grief claws at the edges of my senses and I am barely able to keep it at bay. Looking down at my feet to avoid spotting Meg and my mother's broken bodies, I don't notice the flash of iron until it is too late. Helene's cries morph into another burst of laughter, and she sinks her dagger into my heart with a brutal force.

I stumble backwards and fall, staring up at her only to find my own shock mimicked on her face, her eyes wide and lips parted. And then I see the tip of a dagger protruding from her chest, blood blossoming across her bosom.

In a second, she falls to the ground, the knife slipping away, leaving Meg behind her, my mother's dagger clutched in her hands.

21

The dull ache in my chest seems hardly of consequence. Before me, the very mortal, very magicless, and now very dead Helene lays in the dirt, the same shocked expression on her face.

"Meg?" I look at her, confused, but she wastes no time. Rushing over to me, she desperately calls for my mother.

"Althaea! Althaea, get up, now! Your daughter needs you!"

From my position in the earth, I can just hear the soft moaning of my mother from behind me as she struggles to her feet.

"What? How are you both... alive?"

"It was your magic, my darling. It was you." My mother comes into view, her face proud and weary but full of sharp concentration. She scans me up and down, then whispers urgently to Meg. "Quick. Grab whatever you can find from the bundle that was on the bed, and an iron basin that can sit in coals. We may still be able to save her." She looks back at me, a heartbreaking smile on her face as she smoothes away stray hairs from my face.

"Why are you sad, mother?" I try to shift, but the impact from the blade must have been more powerful than I thought. It hurts. Just gotta heal myself first.

Pressing my fingers to my breast, I summon my light. The warmth fills me, making me whole, and I smile. "See? I'm fine. But... are you alright?"

The second I pull my hands away, the pain returns, doubling in intensity, and I look down to see the wound still deep in my chest, black tar-like blood bubbling around it.

"Mama?" Suddenly a swirl of fear fills me and I look up at her, full of confusion.

Pushing my fingers deep into the wound I once again call upon the magic, filling me up and watch as the cavern closes, pushing my fingers to the surface. But the second I release my magic, the wound reappears, the pain increasing even more. I cry out at the force of it, the strange circumstance, and the confusion I feel.

"What... what happened? Did I lose my power?"

"No, my darling." My mother smiles at me, a small tear trickling down one cheek.

Fuck. This is serious.

Meg's voice chimes in as she rushes to my side. "Helene poisoned the blade. I saw it just as I came to. There was this black oil dripping from the blade, and it looked... evil."

She thrusts the bundle into my mother's hands, and my mother sets to work. I can feel darkness clawing its way through my body, seeking to gain control. It burns and freezes in the worst imaginable way and a voice in my head begs for death to end the pain. I grit my teeth, unwilling to give up, though every second that passes is a new battle worth fighting as the poison climbs through my veins.

Meg slides behind me, cradling my head in her lap, gently tracing fingers across my brow and brushing aside the beads of sweat that develop as I fight to stay alive. "Hello, you." She whispers, and I force an easy smile, but the effort pulls me down into the depths of pain once more. "Ssshh. No. Don't move. Just rest. Althaea will sort you out, you'll see."

My mother flutters about, building a small fire and tossing the herbs into the bowl above the flames. She dashes about, her own signs of exertion dappled across her brow as she works to craft the perfect antidote.

"Do you know what it was that she used?" Meg's voice is quiet, curious but also afraid of the answer.

"I do not. I've never seen anything like this. This isn't hemlock, or nightshade, or even snakeroot. This is…" She trails off, a look of frustration settling over her face. She shakes her head, and resumes her task, eyes furrowing once more in concentration. "I'm a healer. I will heal her."

Mixing and smashing, she darts frequent glances at the black ooze weeping from my chest, bubbling slightly with every labored beat of my heart. "Mama…" I whisper. "Mama, I can't…"

"I know, my darling. I'm working as fast as I can."

She makes a few last adjustments and sits back. Closing her eyes, raising her face to the sky, her lips move quickly, a rapid prayer being sent to the heavens. Then she sinks her hands into the hot, sap-like liquid, wincing in pain, and collects as much as she can carry. Looking deeply into my eyes, she nods firmly. "Are you ready?"

I can see her skin turning red by the second, tiny pustules erupting from her skin with the scorching heat of the sticky substance. Reaching blindly above me, I grasp for Meg's hand, and she grips it firmly. I nod quickly, hoping the pain will at least keep me lucid, fully pushing away the awful sense of death that threatens to silence me forever.

Opening her hands, she holds them above my heart, the thick ooze slowly dripping down from her palms. It is amber, like the eyes of my princess, with tiny bubbles mired in its heavy weight.
When the pus reaches my skin, the pain rockets through me like a lightning bolt and I can barely keep myself awake. Fighting every synapse firing in my brain, begging me to rest, I focus on the pain, feeling it acutely, waiting for it to fade and mend the wound.

Time ticks on, and the black hole seems to swallow the medicine whole. The pain does not end, and my mother's face morphs into one of dire frustration.

"What is it? What's happening?" Meg's voice floats over my shoulder, panic ringing with every syllable.

"It isn't working. The poison is magical. She must have poisoned the blade before her powers were destroyed."

"Magical?"

Their words float over me, muffled sounds like someone's hands are covering my ears. I struggle to sit up, to see what's happening, but my mother pushes down on my chest, eyes boring into me with the intensity of a mother's glare. I almost laugh at the sight of it. And then... I faint.

*****

My mother is calling me. Shuffling my feet closer to my body, I press myself as far back against the wall of our cottage as I can, hoping the wispy thicket of branches disguise my form. She calls again, the level of frustration building in her voice. If she finds me... I'll be in trouble.

I watch as her feet crunch along the gravel path not even three feet from my hiding spot, holding my breath. And then, her feet stop moving.

"There you are."

She reaches out and plucks me up by my hand; how she saw it I'll never know, but with the surety of rain she finds me every time. "What's this?" Her eyes go wide as she sees the gaping wound on my leg, a deep scratch I got while playing in her herb house.

I shake my head, floppy bangs swishing gently across my forehead as I bite my lip to keep my secret. I shouldn't have been in there. I'm going to be in trouble.

"Where did you get this? How did you get hurt?" Her eyes are cross, and I look to the ground, a feeling of dread welling up into my stomach. The wound is burning, painful. But I've never been afraid of pain. What I'm truly afraid of... is the disappointment in her eyes.

"That's it, then." She tugs on my hand, pulling me along behind her as we walk back towards the herb house and she flings open the door. Short noises slip through pursed lips as she checks every plant and bundle, dipping her head low and rising onto her tiptoes in order to carefully observe the room. And then she sees it; the small bundle of wickerbark with a subtle sheen of blood across the edges. "Do you know what this is?" She points to the bundle that so wounded me, pinching her forehead. "While it may appear harmless, wickerbark is a powerful poison, grown only by dark magicians. I only have some so

as to brew an antidote, and here you are... climbing around like a little mountain goat and ignorantly trying to send yourself to your death!"

With a loud roar of frustration, she spins on her heel, glare pinning me to my spot by the door. Sitting me down, she immediately grabs a basin and busies herself plucking various items from around the room. Mixing them in the bowl, she stares at me, pulling her knife from the hip holster under her skirt. "Look at me, Alina. I want you to learn your lesson this time." And then she draws the dagger across her skin.

A gasp parts my tiny lips as shimmering drops of blood drip down into the bowl. The mixture clouds to a murky brown, a concoction of vile consistency and appearance.

Scooping the sludge up with her spoon, she holds it out in front of me. "Every healing requires a sacrifice. In almost every instance, it is only energy. But every once in a while... when the very root of evil grows within... the essence of life itself must be given, in order to reverse the damage done." Holding my gaze steady, she coats the wound with the remedy, and the pain vanishes instantly.

Bursting into tears, I wail and cry, fears from so many things surging through my little six-year-old body, and my mother gathers me into her arms, kissing the top of my hair.

"There, there... little one. It is alright now. All will be well." She sits there, holding me as the sun sinks below the horizon, until my cries still and I fall asleep in her arms.

*****

I gasp and my eyes fly open, bringing me back to the present, and I gulp in the oxygen. "Blood!" I barely get the word out between my heaving breaths. "It needs... a sacrifice."

"The blood!" The words are a whisper, but they ring out clear as day. And just as my mother's eyes scan the crater in which we stand, Meg lunges forward, grabs my mother's dagger, and pulls it across her wrist in one clean stroke.

The blood bursts forth like a quickly blooming flower, spurting in a geyser up into the air and falling like rain. Holding her arm over me, she leans down above my face, a beautiful smile on her perfect lips.

Three warm, soft drops land gently like snowflakes into the wound and all at once, color returns to my sight, crisp sounds fall upon my ears, and the world comes back into focus, senses bursting into the fullness of their abilities in one magical second. My flesh rises, knitting itself together once more, and my heart roars to life within me, a surge of energy bursting through my veins.

I can hear a squeal of delight, and then Meg's arms are wrapped around me, her laughter ringing out through the air like crisp silver bells. Tears slide down her cheeks and she rocks us back and forth with energy and happiness.

Overwhelmed at her joy, a grin breaks out across my face, and I slide a palm across her cheek, pulling her face to mine. Our kiss is salty and sweet, warm and decadent... it is, without a doubt, the kiss I have been waiting for my whole life.

When our lips finally part, I wrap my hand around her wrist, feeling the magic flow between us, binding her flesh together. Then bringing my lips to her wrist, I kiss the brand-new skin, wishing to be the first to touch it.

Finally I pull away from her and stretch my fingers out towards my mother, the sparkling golden glow twisting through the air and looping around her hands, restoring the soft, smooth skin. No more burns, no more blisters, just the hands that have healed so many over the years.

The three of us melt together in a hug of relief and joy, and there we remain, weeping and whispering our thanksgivings.

"Goddess be praised. Alina, my darling, you are brilliant!"

Meg leans back, eyes flying open. "Alina? Your name... is Alina?"

I groan in good humor, smiling at her. "I suppose it's time you knew, isn't it?"

Meg's smile is as bright as the sun above us, and her pink cheeks flush a deeper shade, this final barrier between us broken down. Pulling us back into another hug, she squeezes us tightly.

Once our joints are sore and stiff from holding each other for so long, we rise, and I cannot help the bark of laughter that escapes my lips.

"We are quite the sight!" I exclaim. Looking between us my grin widens until all three of us are laughing. Hairs a frazzled mess, clothes tattered, torn, and singed, dirt and soot across our faces, and a giant black hole just over my breast, sticky black tar now dried into my clothes.

Meg's eyes are no longer on our bedraggled forms anymore. Instead, she looks to the outline of the castle, looming far off in the distance.

"Meg?" My mother asks. "Are you alright?"

"It's time to go home. It's time to tell my father."

22

I tug at the leather strap, tightening my satchel close to my hip. The sheer weight of the coins in my pocket is almost indecent, but I'm no fool. I'll need them.

Looking around, I gaze at the bustle of the castle. A month has passed, and while the king's fear of magic is still strong, he realizes he would not be alive without it. The involvement of magic is a closely guarded secret, and not even the king's closest advisors know what truly took place. Gormliath is preparing for a peace summit. Leaders from each of the seven sacred kingdoms are set to descend upon the castle in only a few short weeks, with talks of re-establishing the Great Empire. The king is now healed, thanks to me; Helene's poisons only a ghost in his system. Meg's been busy; so busy, in fact, that I've barely seen her. The future Queen of Gormliath has a lot of catching up to do if she is to rule someday.

With the gossip mill still ripe with talk of curses, I know it is best to keep my secret for now. I work alongside my mother as a simple healer, learning more and more of the antidotes, bone settings, and medicine of our time. It isn't easy, and I find it honorable work but... I am restless.

Sighing, I push off the wall and look to the small collection of belongings I have tucked away for myself, and then my eyes drift to the letter that lays upon them.

"I'll be back in a bit." I bid farewell to my mother and step out into the city, walking along the high street towards the castle gate. This time, the guards let me in without hesitation, and my heart twists strangely at the development.

I make my way to the kitchens and find one of the serving maids bustling to prepare the evening meal. "Excuse me. Would you please see that this gets to Princess Meg?"

She looks up at me in alarm, then smiles when she recognizes me. "Oh, I certainly will!"

Handing it to her, I nod abruptly and turn to go. I can hear her giggles mix with those of other servants as they stare at the cover of the letter. "Oh, she's written the princess a love letter! Isn't this romantic?"

Cringing, I duck out the door as quickly as I can, a mixture of shame and embarrassment flooding my cheeks.

When I return to the house, my mother greets me at the door. Her eyes are sad, and I find myself unwilling to look at her. But then I feel her hands slide along my cheek, and she gently kisses my head. "Let's get you packed."

We bundle the items slowly, and my mother takes each piece in her hands and touches it gently as if it is made of glass. New clothes from Uma and Enora, bread and vegetables for days, and my mother's precious dagger, now mine, all fitted into their rightful places.

My mother helps me slide into a soft wool cloak and pulls the hood up over my head, tugging it down around my chin. She looks into my eyes lovingly and clicks her tongue against her teeth.

"Are you sure you don't want to say goodbye?"

I nod abruptly and place my hands over hers. "You don't need to worry about me."

"Ah, but my darling. That's what mothers do." She smiles at me, with a hint of sadness pushing against the corners of her mouth.

Letting go of my cloak, she takes my hand and leads me outside. We walk together in silence until we reach the edge of town, the tall gate opening to the long road that stretches into the open countryside. Turning to look at her and the city behind me, I feel an ache in my heart. "You'll take care of them, won't you? All of them?"

She smiles deeply and squeezes my hand. "You know that I will." Pressing a hand against my chest, she taps her fingers twice. "It's in our blood."

Turning her eyes to the horizon, she squints into the late afternoon sun as the giant glowing orb begins a slow descent. "You'd better get a move on. It'll be dark in just a few hours."

Looking at her, I pull her into a hug. "I'll be back."

"I know."

"I love you."

"And I love you."

She kisses me once more, then lets go of my hand and walks away, disappearing into the crowded streets. Closing my eyes, I take a deep breath, and take my first step.

"That's an awfully despicable thing to do, you know." A voice comes out of nowhere.

I gasp and swirl towards the sound, noticing a figure disguised under a heavy dark hood leaning against the stone wall. For a minute, my stomach turns with fear, but then I realize how small and delicate the frame is and the voice suddenly clicks in my mind.

"Did you really think I would let you go just like that?" Meg's voice is both amused and annoyed. "Honestly, Alina! You trying to be noble is the biggest pain in my ass! Constantly thinking I'm too busy to spend time with you, or refusing to consider the fact that I might have an inkling of what is going through your thick head? Can you stop being you for a damn second?"

I sigh in defeat and smile ruefully at her. "I guess you figured me out."

"Long before your note," she says, marching over to me and throwing back her hood. "I'm no fool."

"I know that." I try and agree with her but she scowls at me with a fire in her eyes.

"Then you should know better than to think I would simply let you leave with nothing but a sorry excuse of a note saying farewell." With a final glare, she sets her jaw and stares me down. "Now as your princess,

I command you to follow me." And with that, she stomps off in another direction.

"You're not actually my princess!" I call after her. "I'm not a citizen of Gormliath!"

"Just follow me, you stubborn woman!"

With an exasperated laugh, I move along behind her, my long strides quickly catching me up. Not far off, the woods loom over us, and I see Curaidh tethered to a sturdy, low-hanging branch. "What's all this?"

"Transportation!" She beams at me proudly. "Did you really think I would let us walk everywhere and leave this gorgeous boy behind?" She preens at the horse, nuzzling her face into the side of his neck.

"I didn't expect you to-" I cut myself off, realizing what she said. "We? What do you mean, we?"

Placing her hands on her hips, she straightens her spine and stands as tall as her tiny frame can muster. "I'm coming with you, of course. To think that you would believe that I would simply let you walk away from all that we have been through, and that I would give up on all that you are to me?"

I open my mouth in retort but she storms ahead, lifting a hand to silence me. "As I told you once before, not only are you a scoundrel, but you're incredibly daft too!"

I blink at her, my brain failing to grasp how she could be so irresponsible. "You can't come with me! You're to be the new queen. You have people to serve and a job to do - literally, the most important job in the kingdom, and you were born for this!"

She laughs giddily, a mischievous sparkle in her eye. "No, my darling I was not. And I'm not going to become the future queen."

"You're... not?" The details are coming in too fast, and I blink at her rapidly, confused.

"My father and I spoke, and I'm abdicating my place. Thanks to you, he is well and has many years ahead of him. And he has good counsel in your mother. He listens to her and he trusts her. She's helping him."

Stepping towards me, she takes my hands in hers, lightly tracing circles across my palm with her soft, tender fingertips.

"I want to be with you. Not married to some noble, not tied to tradition. I was never meant to lead, anyway. Twelfth in line, I was left more to entertain myself by keeping out of trouble than to understand court politics and international affairs. I don't want to be Queen. And I have no interest in forcing you to live this life when you so clearly have no desire to live it either. I want you, and a life with you, whatever that may mean - because I love you."

She bends down and picks up a heavy satchel and holds it out to me. "Now are you going to help me or not?"

With a grin that stretches across my face, I take it from her and toss it over Curaidh's back then drop into a low bow. "Then, my lady... will you do me the honor of accepting my company?"

"Yes... Yes!" She flies towards me, and I swoop down, scooping her up in my arms and pulling her tight. My fingers slide along her waist and up her sides, and when she opens her eyes to look at me, I kiss her with all of the love and happiness I feel inside.

She blushes crimson, a rush of heat just below the skin and it is so thrilling that I find myself drawn to the sensation, wanting to see it again and again. And so I clear my throat and prepare to admit the words out loud that have never slipped past my lips.

"Meg..." I push back a lock of her hair, twirling it between my fingers. "When you were hurt... when I thought you were dead- I was... well, it ruined me. I couldn't take it. I wanted to kill Helene. It was all I could think to do. Somehow... I didn't. Somehow I stopped myself. But I have never felt this level of fear before. I can't- I don't-"

The more I ramble on, the more I realize I am beginning to make no sense. To make matters worse, Meg holds her hand drawn into a half fist in front of her lips, barely concealing the giddy and understanding smile on her face.

"You... what?" She goads me on, her eyes wrinkling with mirth, and I growl a little in half-hearted frustration.

"I love you!" The words burst from my lips and I stand there, stunned.

Oh... my... goddess. That's how I said it? I practically shouted it at her! Actually, I did shout it at her, and in an angry voice!

Meg bursts out laughing, cackling at me as she doubles over, clutching at her waist. She pushes her hair out of her face and rights herself, eyes squinting shut with the force of her laughter.

I stand there, gaping at her, mortified and amused all at once. Finally she stumbles over to me and throws her arms around me, pulling me close. "Come here, you absolute disaster."

And then she kisses me, just long enough to clear my mind of the world around us, but still I wish it would go on. I shift my head, every intention in my mind to kiss her again from another angle, and she giggles and whispers against my mouth. "You're my favorite disaster, though."

"As long as I'm your only disaster..." And I capture her lips again.

This time, our kiss dissolves into giggles before it can go much further and she perches up on her tiptoes, placing a peck on the tip of my nose.

"I love you too."

"I know."

She nips at my bottom lip, giving me a teasingly defiant glare that sends my stomach into somersaults. "Do you?"

"I do. I knew that the second you spilled your blood in order to save mine. Or maybe I've known longer. Maybe I've known since the moment you stormed into that stable, wondering if it were really me."

"And I've known you loved me since the day you saved my Curaidh."

"Is that so?" I squeeze her sides gently and she shivers under my touch, grinning, then looks deeply into my eyes.

She scrunches up her nose as she thinks deeply, and then sighs. "Or maybe I've loved you all along. And maybe you've loved me. And somehow... with this whole story we find ourselves in, maybe we were made to love each other long ago."

"Made to save the world long ago?" I tease her, not one to believe in fairy tales... and yet, here I am, living in one. "I suppose there's only one way to find out."

"Find out what?"

"To find out if we're destined to be together, part of a story written long ago."

"What is the one way?" Her amber eyes sparkle with curiosity, and she leans in closer.

Bending down, I whisper into her ear, my lips just brushing against her skin. "Stay with me forever."

"Only if you can catch me!" Grabbing Curaidh's reins, she leaps up onto his back and I barely scramble up in time. Laughing, she reaches back and kisses me on the cheek. "Now... where to first?"

The End.

www.ingramcontent.com/pod-product-compliance
Lightning Source LLC
Chambersburg PA
CBHW061215210726

48294CB00006B/1844